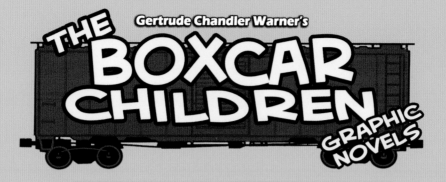

Gertrude Chandler Warner's
THE BOXCAR CHILDREN
GRAPHIC NOVELS

BOOK FIVE
MIKE'S MYSTERY

Henry, Jessie, Violet, and Benny are on summer trip out West, and they're thrilled to find their friend Mike Wood lives in the bustling new town near Mystery Ranch.

But one night a house burns down, and young Mike is blamed for starting the fire! The Boxcar Children know he didn't do it. Can they help their friend?

THE BOXCAR CHILDREN
GRAPHIC NOVELS

1. THE BOXCAR CHILDREN
2. SURPRISE ISLAND
3. THE YELLOW HOUSE MYSTERY
4. MYSTERY RANCH
5. MIKE'S MYSTERY
6. BLUE BAY MYSTERY

Gertrude Chandler Warner's

THE BOXCAR CHILDREN
MIKE'S MYSTERY

Adapted by Christopher E. Long
Illustrated by Mike Dubisch

Henry Alden

Jessie Alden

Watch

Violet Alden

Benny Alden

magic
wagon

Visit us at www.abdopublishing.com

Published by Magic Wagon, a division of the ABDO Group, 8000 West 78th Street,
Edina, Minnesota 55439. Copyright © 2009 by Abdo Consulting Group, Inc.
International copyrights reserved in all countries. All rights reserved.
No part of this book may be reproduced in any form without written permission
from the publisher. Graphic Planet™ is a trademark and logo of Magic Wagon.
This edition produced by arrangement with Albert Whitman & Company.
THE BOXCAR CHILDREN is a registered trademark of Albert Whitman &
Company. www.albertwhitman.com

Adapted by Christopher E. Long
Illustrated by Mike Dubisch
Colored by Wes Hartman
Lettered by Johnny Lowe
Edited by Stephanie Hedlund
Interior layout and design by Kristen Fitzner Denton
Cover art by Mike Dubisch
Book design and packaging by Shannon Eric Denton

Library of Congress Cataloging-in-Publication Data

Long, Christopher E.
  Mike's mystery / adapted by Christopher E. Long ; illustrated by Mike Dubisch.
    p. cm. -- (Gertrude Chandler Warner's boxcar children)
  ISBN 978-1-60270-590-6
  [1. Orphans--Fiction. 2. Family--Fiction. 3. Mystery and detective stories.] I.
Dubisch, Michael, ill. II. Warner, Gertrude Chandler, 1890-1979. Mike's mystery.
III. Title.
  PZ7.W887625Mik 2009
  [E]--dc22
                              2008036094

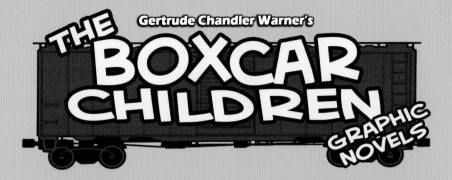

BOOK FIVE

Contents

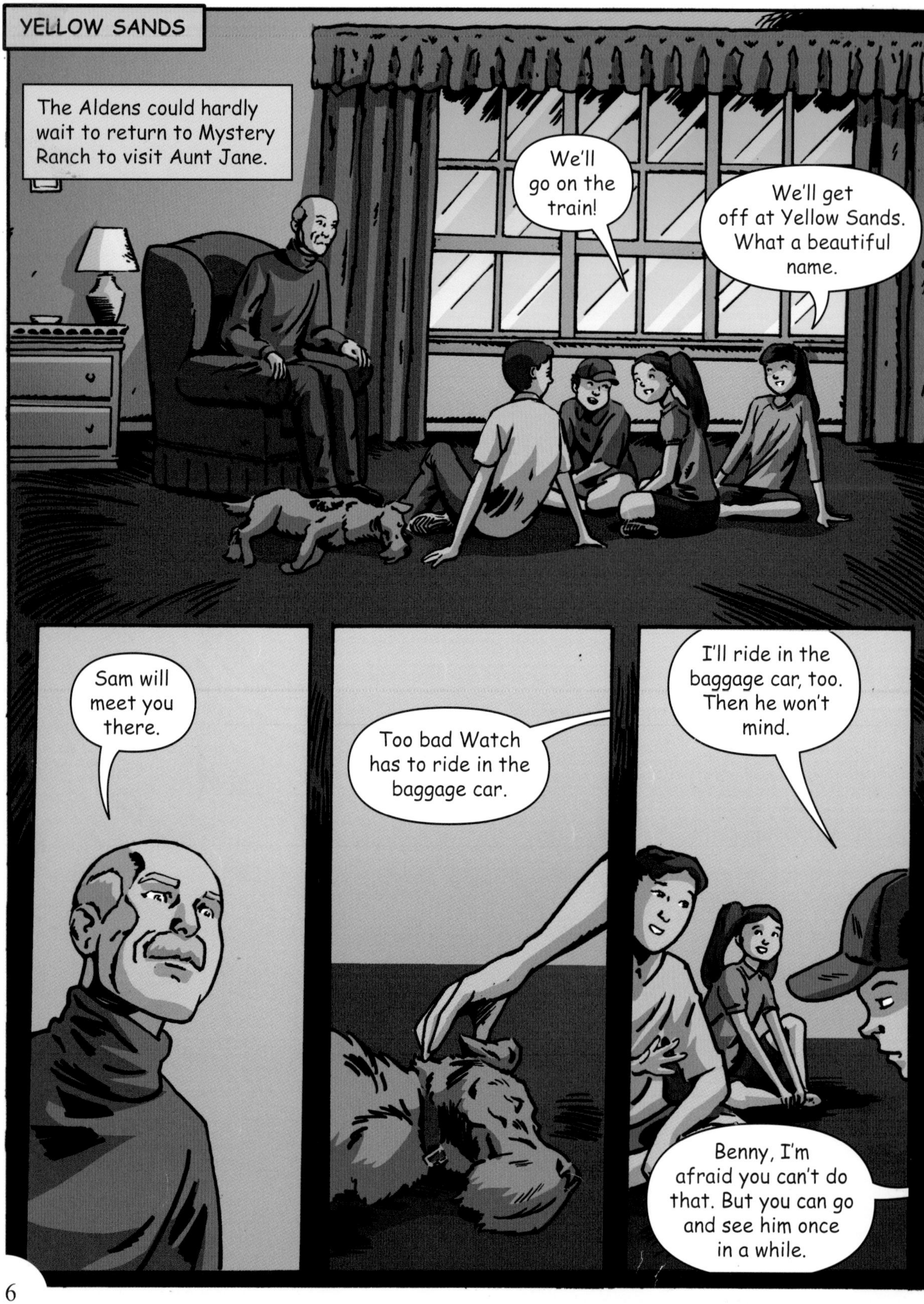
YELLOW SANDS
The Aldens could hardly wait to return to Mystery Ranch to visit Aunt Jane.
We'll go on the train!
We'll get off at Yellow Sands. What a beautiful name.
Sam will meet you there.
Too bad Watch has to ride in the baggage car.
I'll ride in the baggage car, too. Then he won't mind.
Benny, I'm afraid you can't do that. But you can go and see him once in a while.

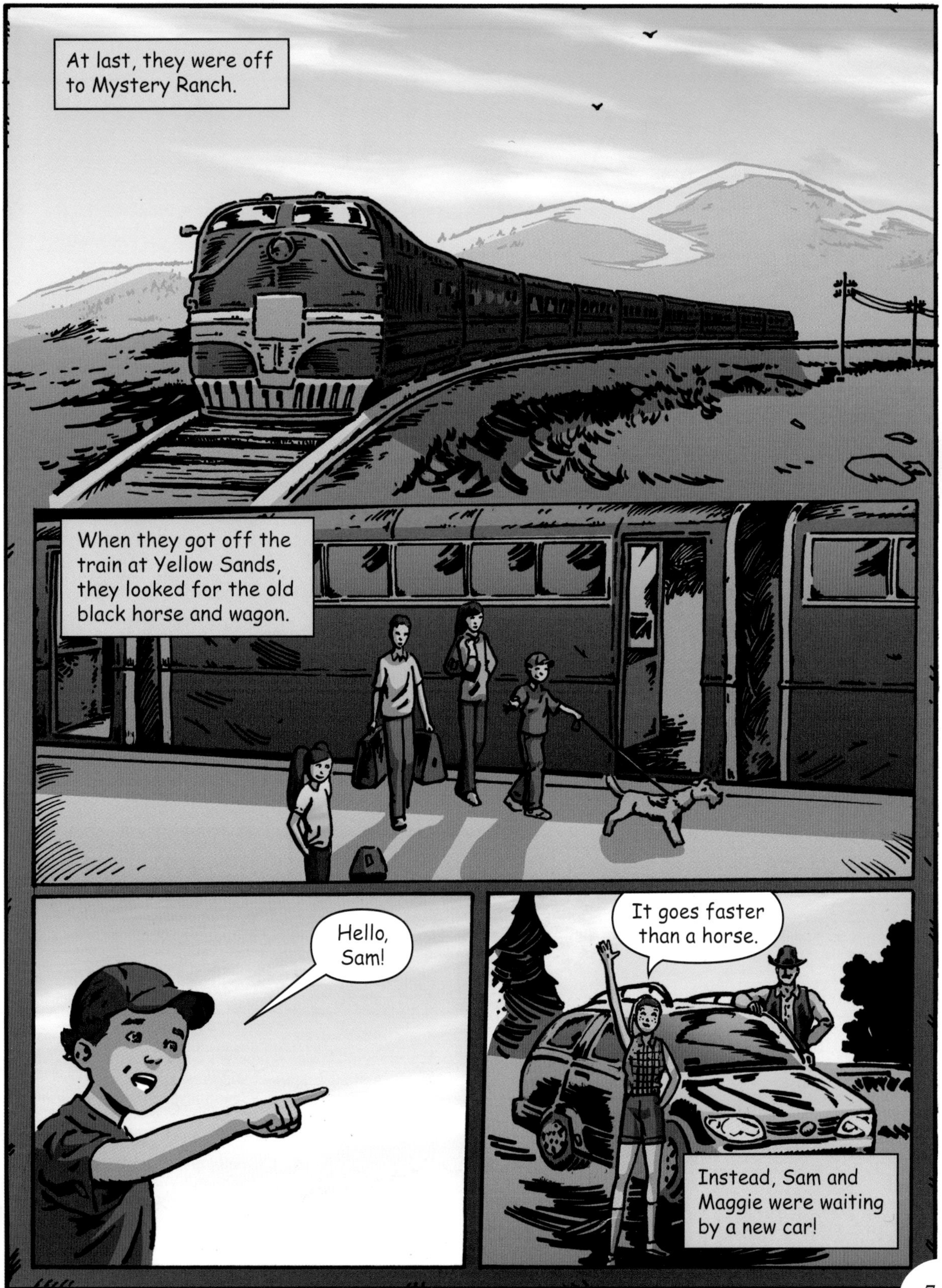
At last, they were off to Mystery Ranch.
When they got off the train at Yellow Sands, they looked for the old black horse and wagon.
Hello, Sam!
It goes faster than a horse.
Instead, Sam and Maggie were waiting by a new car!

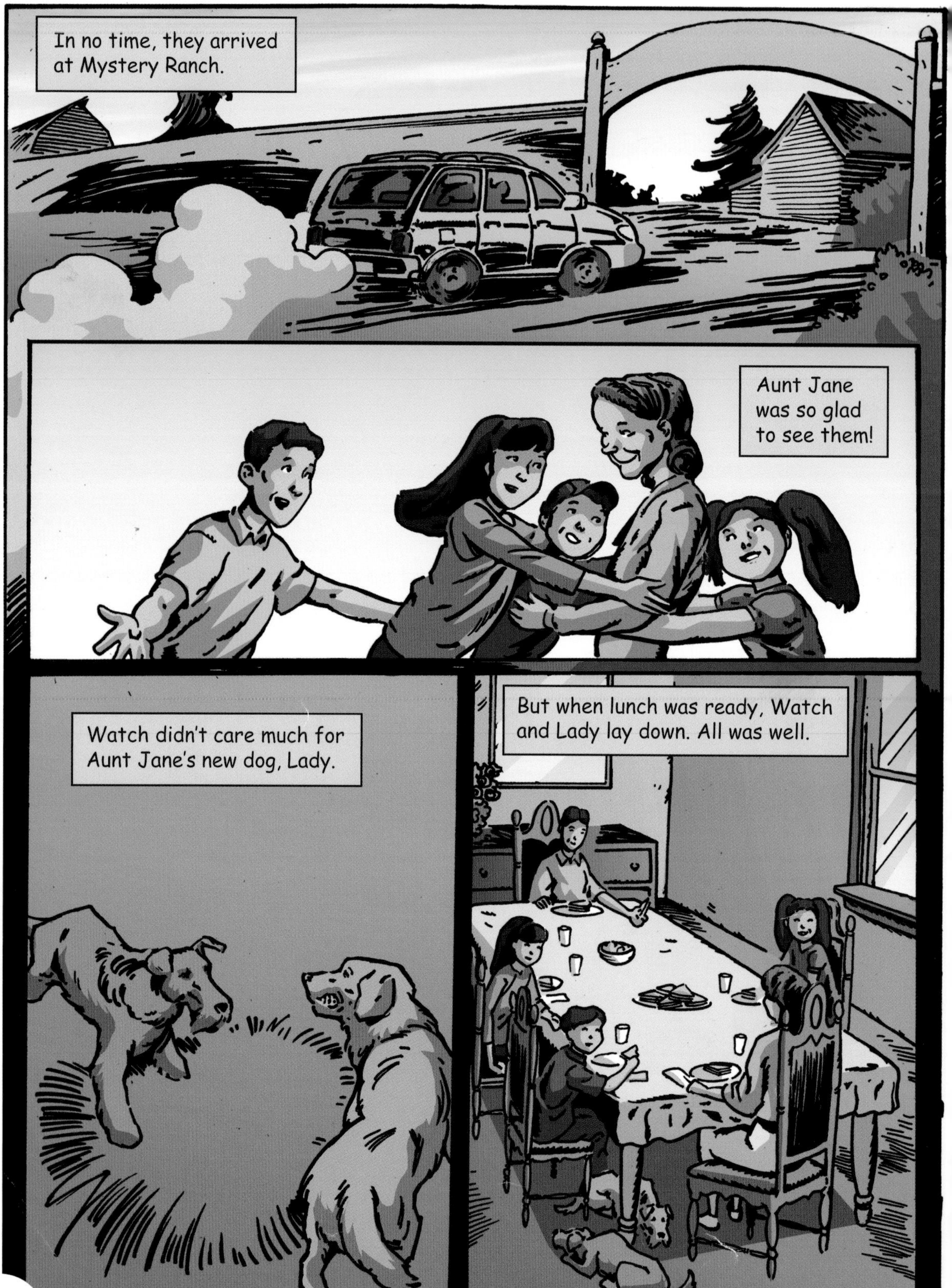
In no time, they arrived at Mystery Ranch.
Aunt Jane was so glad to see them!
Watch didn't care much for Aunt Jane's new dog, Lady.
But when lunch was ready, Watch and Lady lay down. All was well.

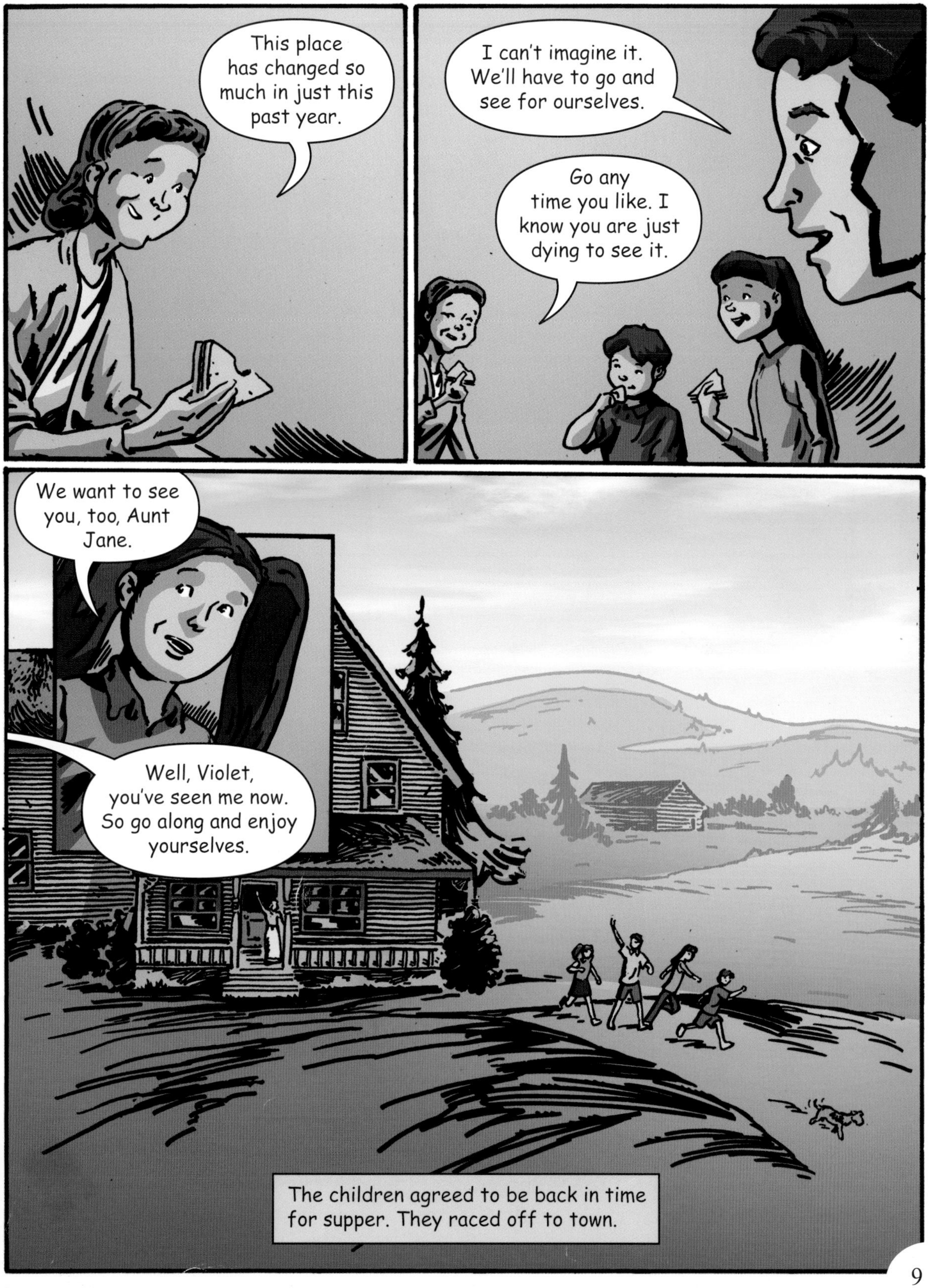

This place has changed so much in just this past year.
I can't imagine it. We'll have to go and see for ourselves.
Go any time you like. I know you are just dying to see it.
We want to see you, too, Aunt Jane.
Well, Violet, you've seen me now. So go along and enjoy yourselves.
The children agreed to be back in time for supper. They raced off to town.

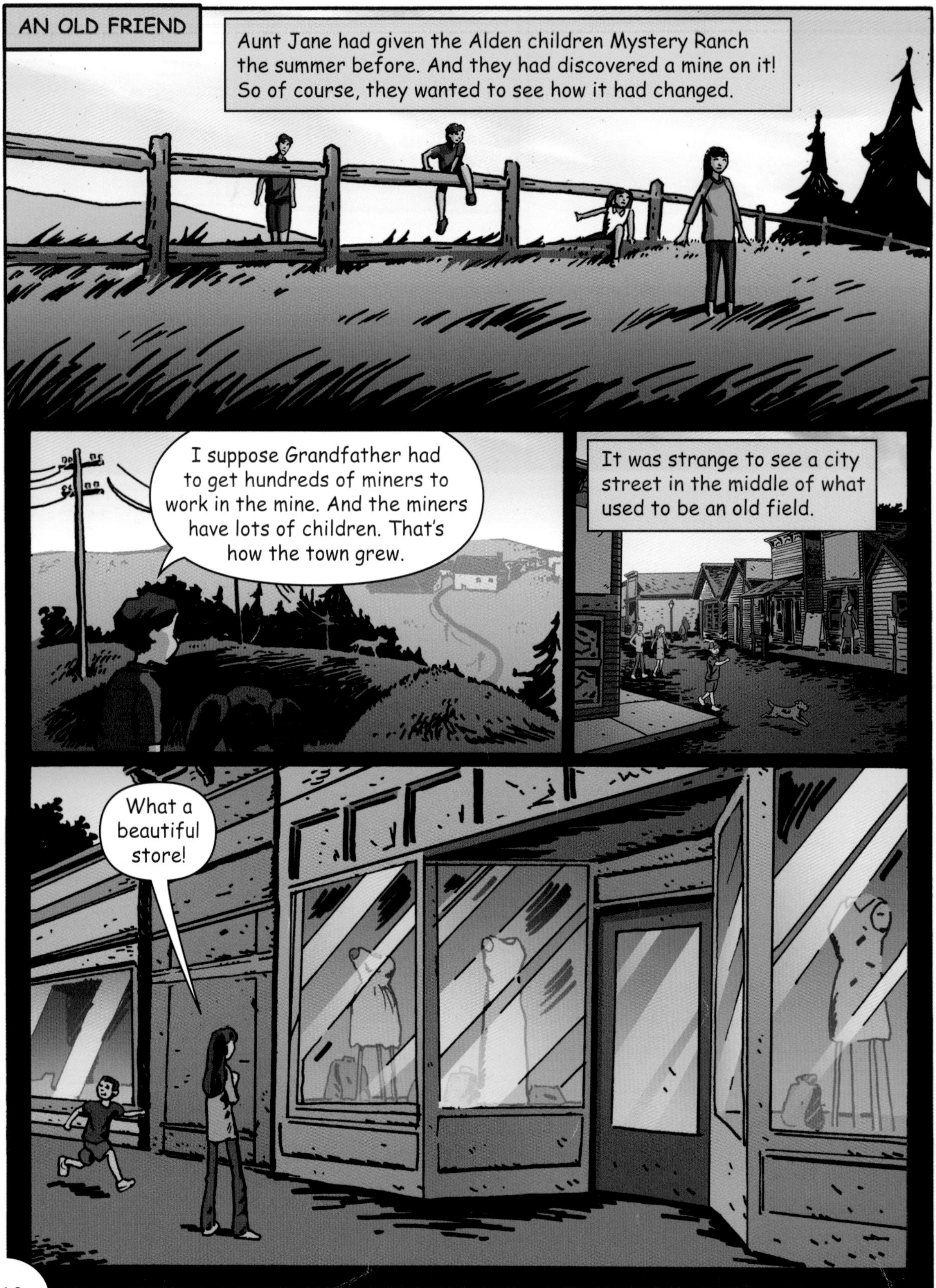
AN OLD FRIEND
Aunt Jane had given the Alden children Mystery Ranch the summer before. And they had discovered a mine on it! So of course, they wanted to see how it had changed.
I suppose Grandfather had to get hundreds of miners to work in the mine. And the miners have lots of children. That's how the town grew.
It was strange to see a city street in the middle of what used to be an old field.
What a beautiful store!

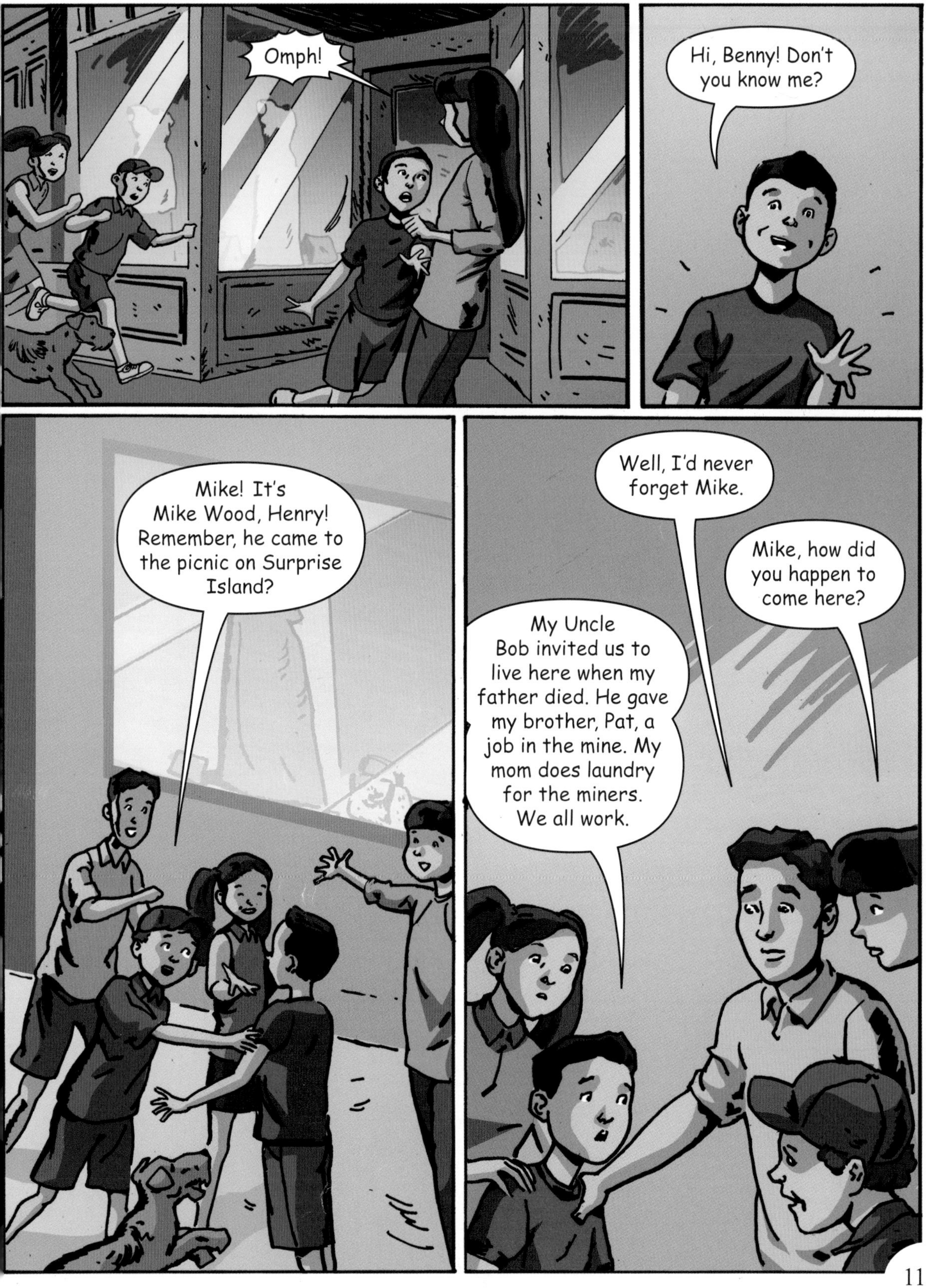

Omph!
Hi, Benny! Don't you know me?
Mike! It's Mike Wood, Henry! Remember, he came to the picnic on Surprise Island?
Well, I'd never forget Mike.
Mike, how did you happen to come here?
My Uncle Bob invited us to live here when my father died. He gave my brother, Pat, a job in the mine. My mom does laundry for the miners. We all work.

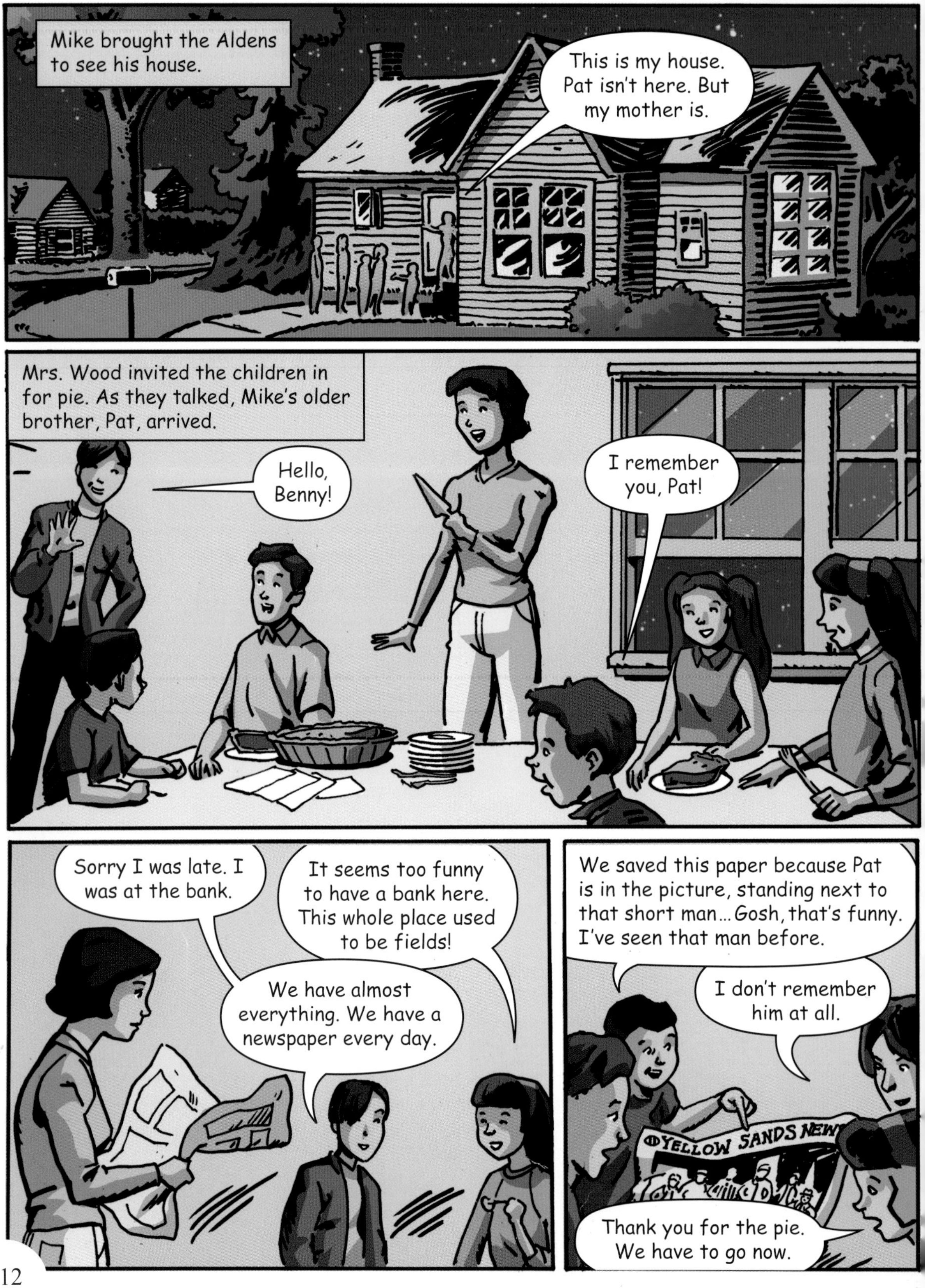
Mike brought the Aldens to see his house.
This is my house. Pat isn't here. But my mother is.
Mrs. Wood invited the children in for pie. As they talked, Mike's older brother, Pat, arrived.
Hello, Benny!
I remember you, Pat!
Sorry I was late. I was at the bank.
It seems too funny to have a bank here. This whole place used to be fields!
We have almost everything. We have a newspaper every day.
We saved this paper because Pat is in the picture, standing next to that short man... Gosh, that's funny. I've seen that man before.
I don't remember him at all.
YELLOW SANDS
Thank you for the pie. We have to go now.

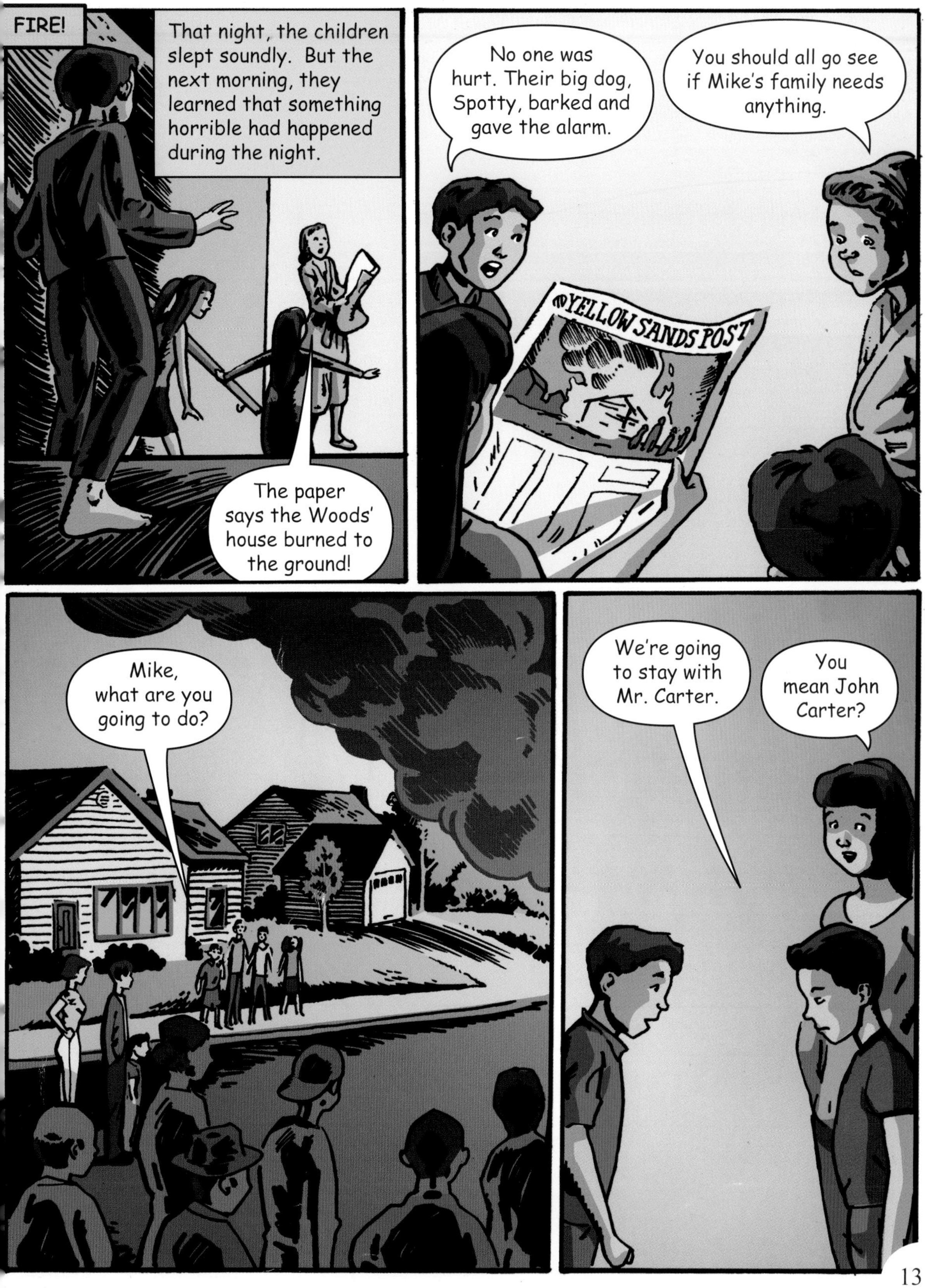
FIRE!
That night, the children slept soundly. But the next morning, they learned that something horrible had happened during the night.
The paper says the Woods' house burned to the ground!
No one was hurt. Their big dog, Spotty, barked and gave the alarm.
You should all go see if Mike's family needs anything.
YELLOW SANDS POST
Mike, what are you going to do?
We're going to stay with Mr. Carter.
You mean John Carter?

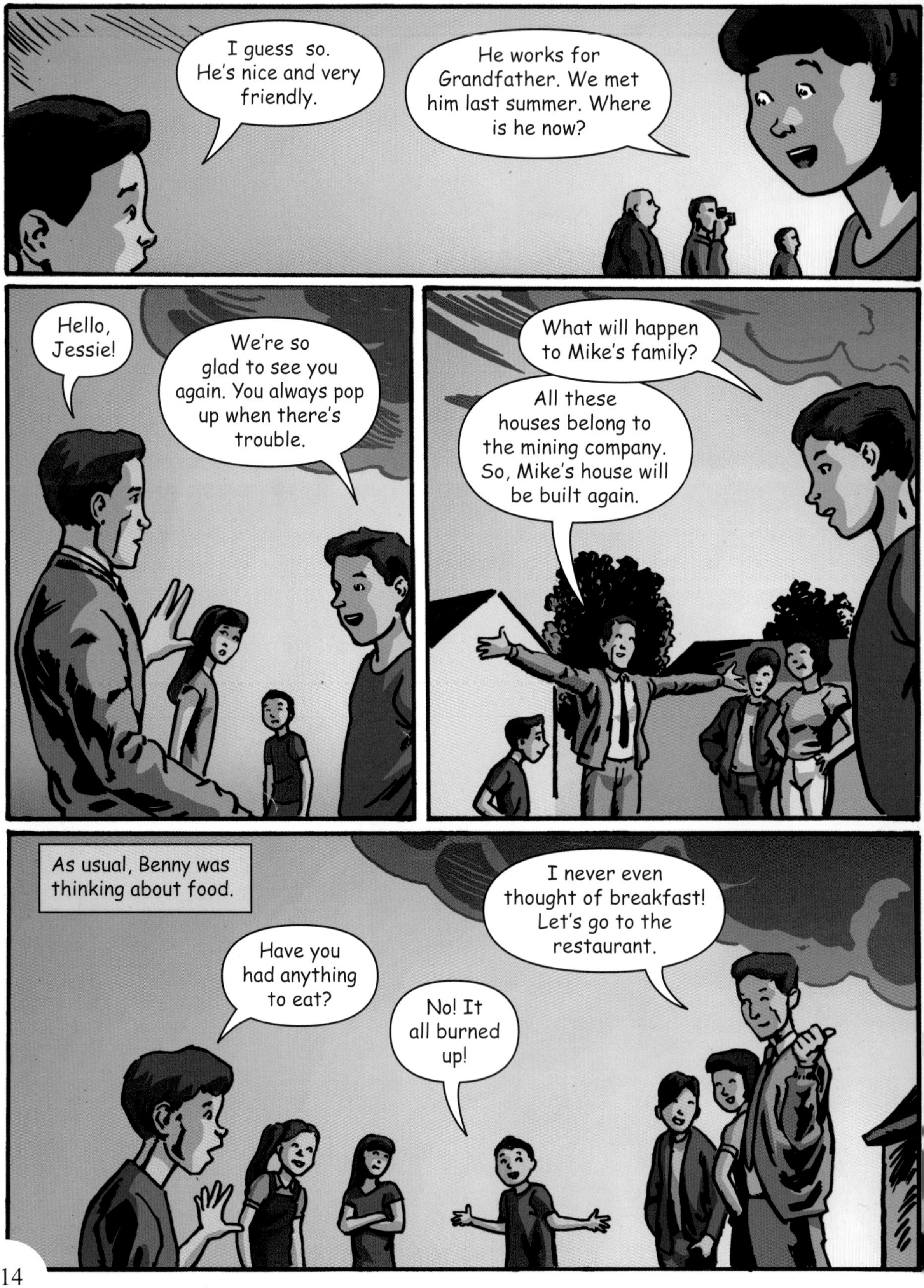

I guess so. He's nice and very friendly.
He works for Grandfather. We met him last summer. Where is he now?
Hello, Jessie!
We're so glad to see you again. You always pop up when there's trouble.
What will happen to Mike's family?
All these houses belong to the mining company. So, Mike's house will be built again.
As usual, Benny was thinking about food.
Have you had anything to eat?
No! It all burned up!
I never even thought of breakfast! Let's go to the restaurant.

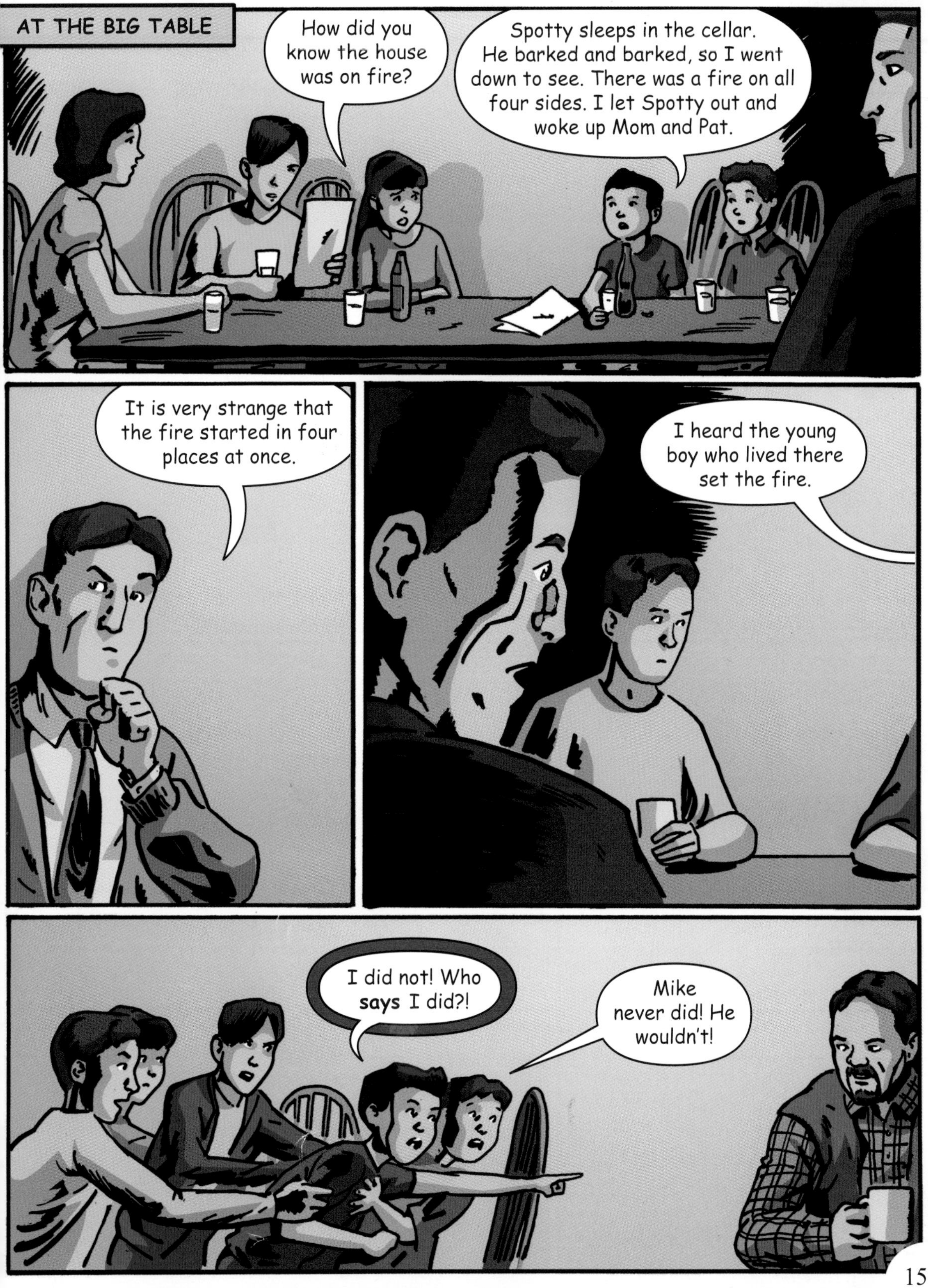
AT THE BIG TABLE
How did you know the house was on fire?
Spotty sleeps in the cellar. He barked and barked, so I went down to see. There was a fire on all four sides. I let Spotty out and woke up Mom and Pat.
It is very strange that the fire started in four places at once.
I heard the young boy who lived there set the fire.
I did not! Who **says** I did?!
Mike never did! He wouldn't!

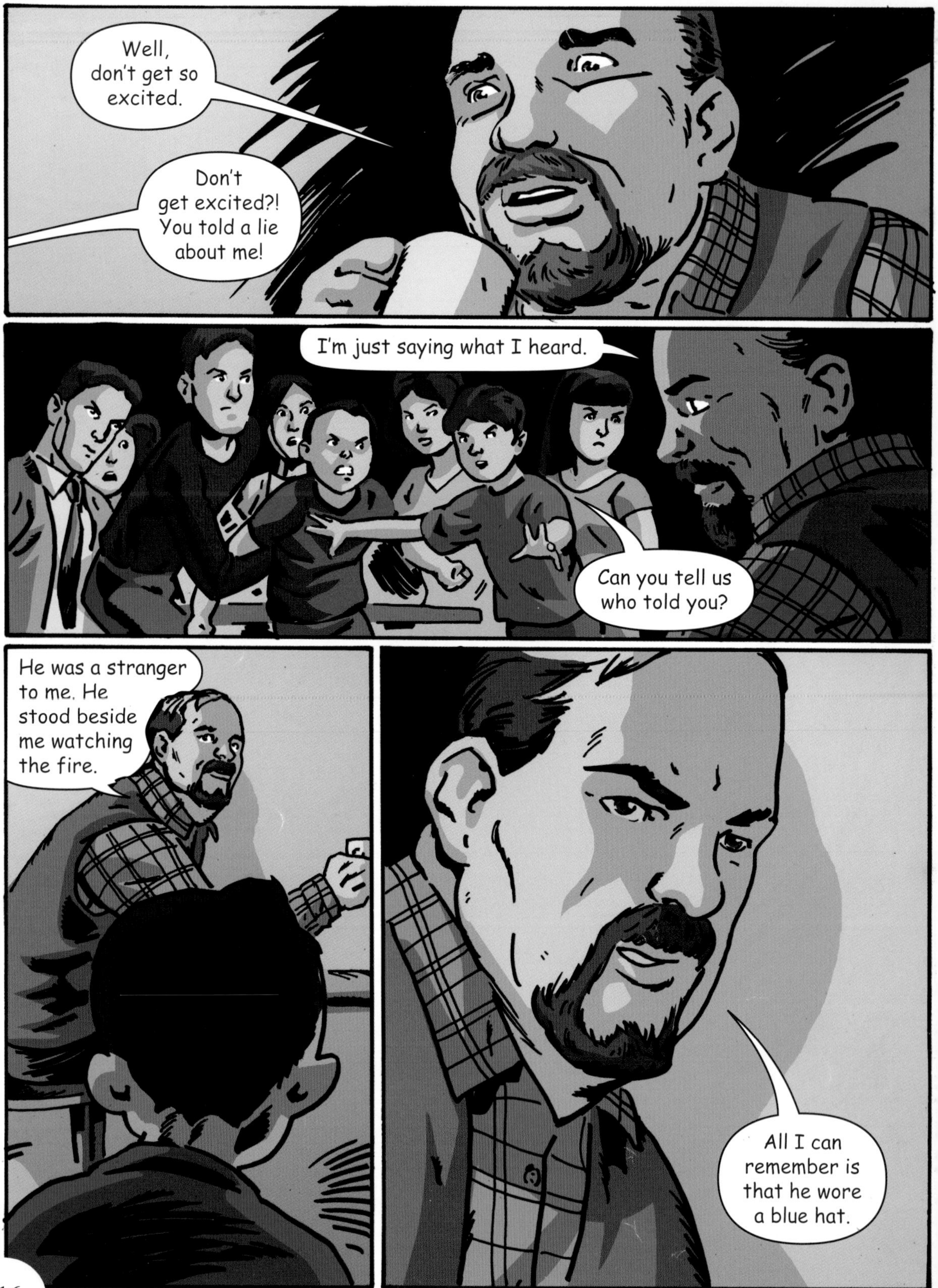
Well, don't get so excited.
Don't get excited?! You told a lie about me!
I'm just saying what I heard.
Can you tell us who told you?
He was a stranger to me. He stood beside me watching the fire.
All I can remember is that he wore a blue hat.

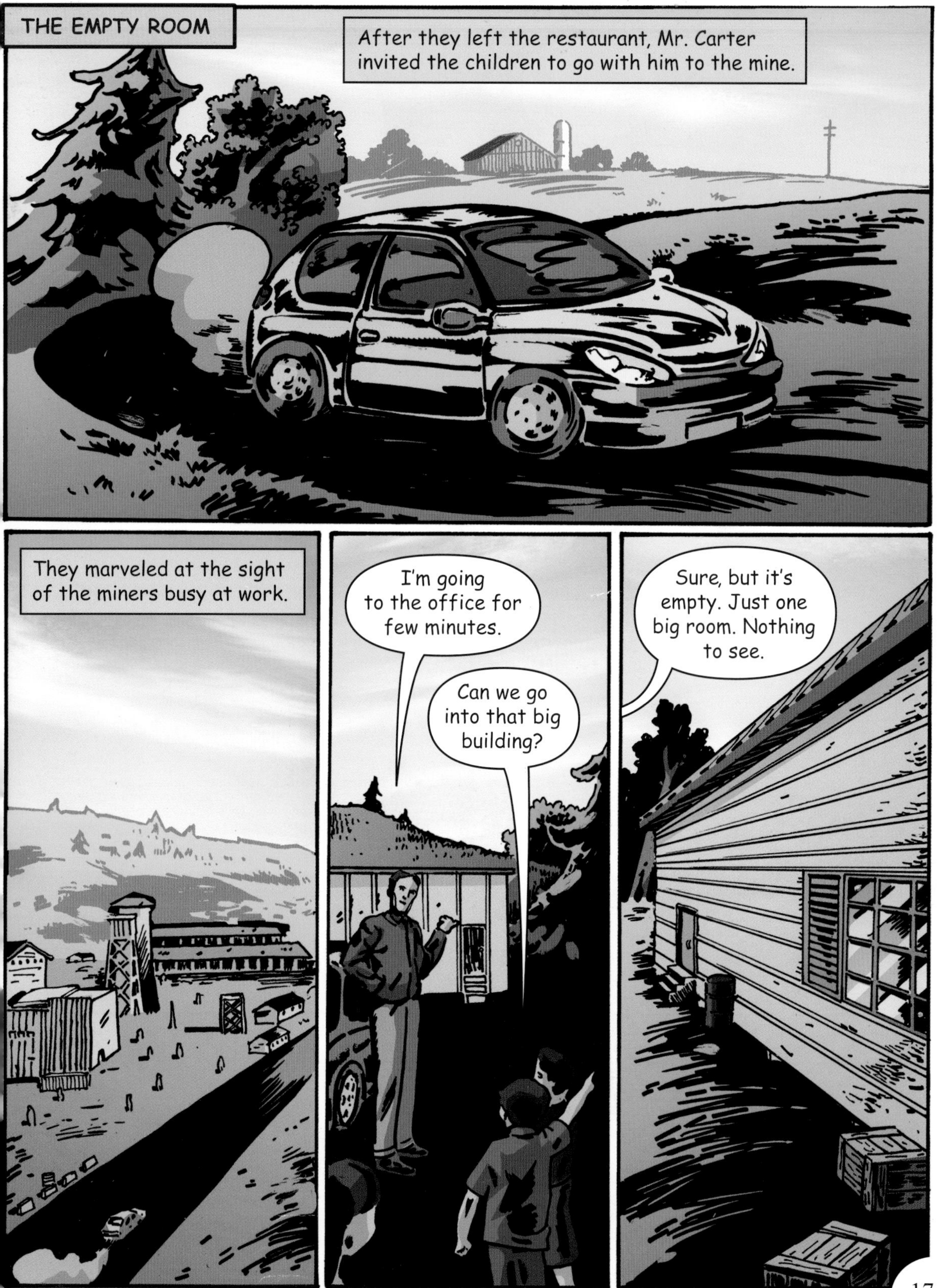
THE EMPTY ROOM
After they left the restaurant, Mr. Carter invited the children to go with him to the mine.
They marveled at the sight of the miners busy at work.
I'm going to the office for few minutes.
Can we go into that big building?
Sure, but it's empty. Just one big room. Nothing to see.

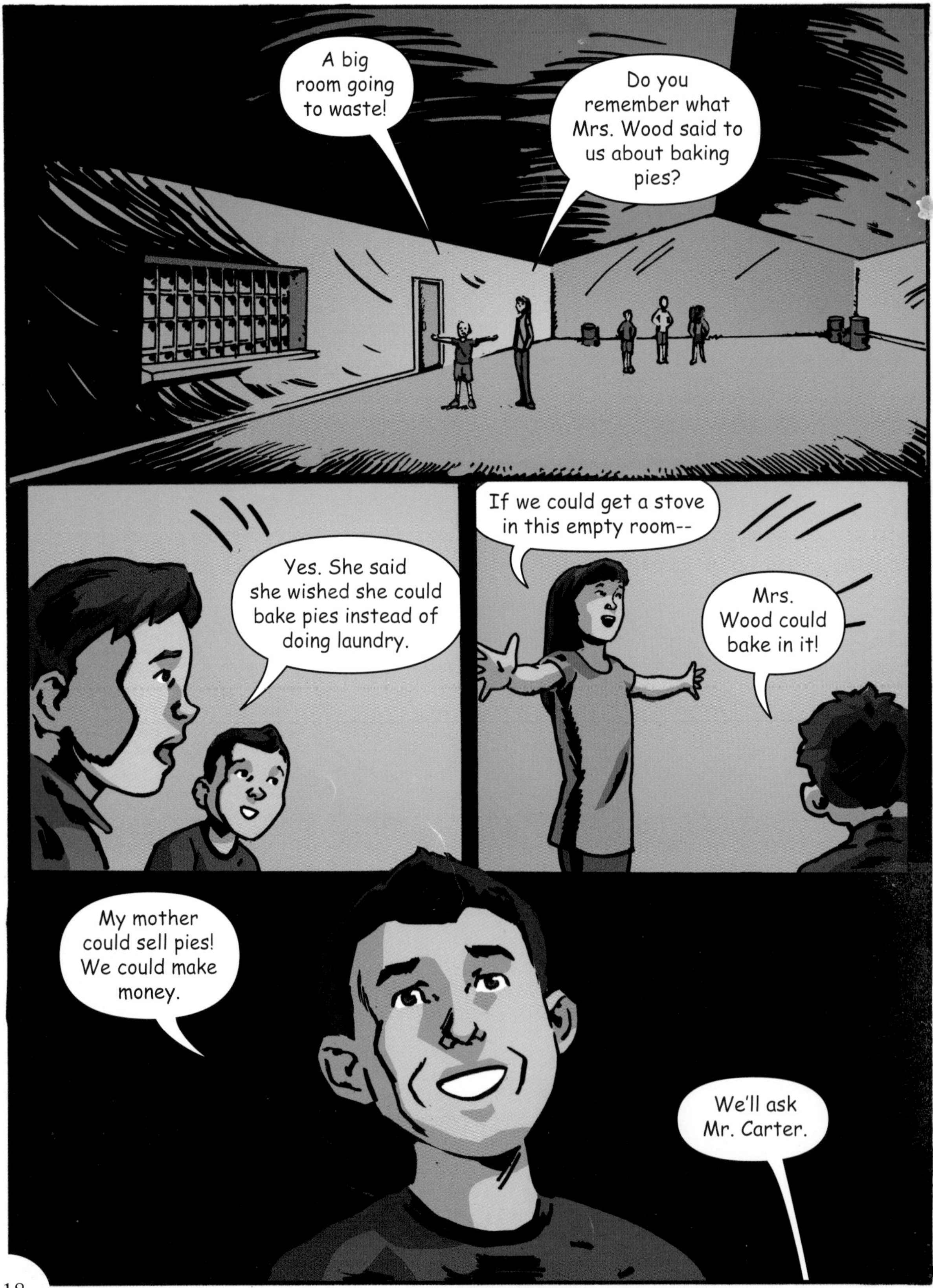
A big room going to waste!
Do you remember what Mrs. Wood said to us about baking pies?
Yes. She said she wished she could bake pies instead of doing laundry.
If we could get a stove in this empty room--
Mrs. Wood could bake in it!
My mother could sell pies! We could make money.
We'll ask Mr. Carter.

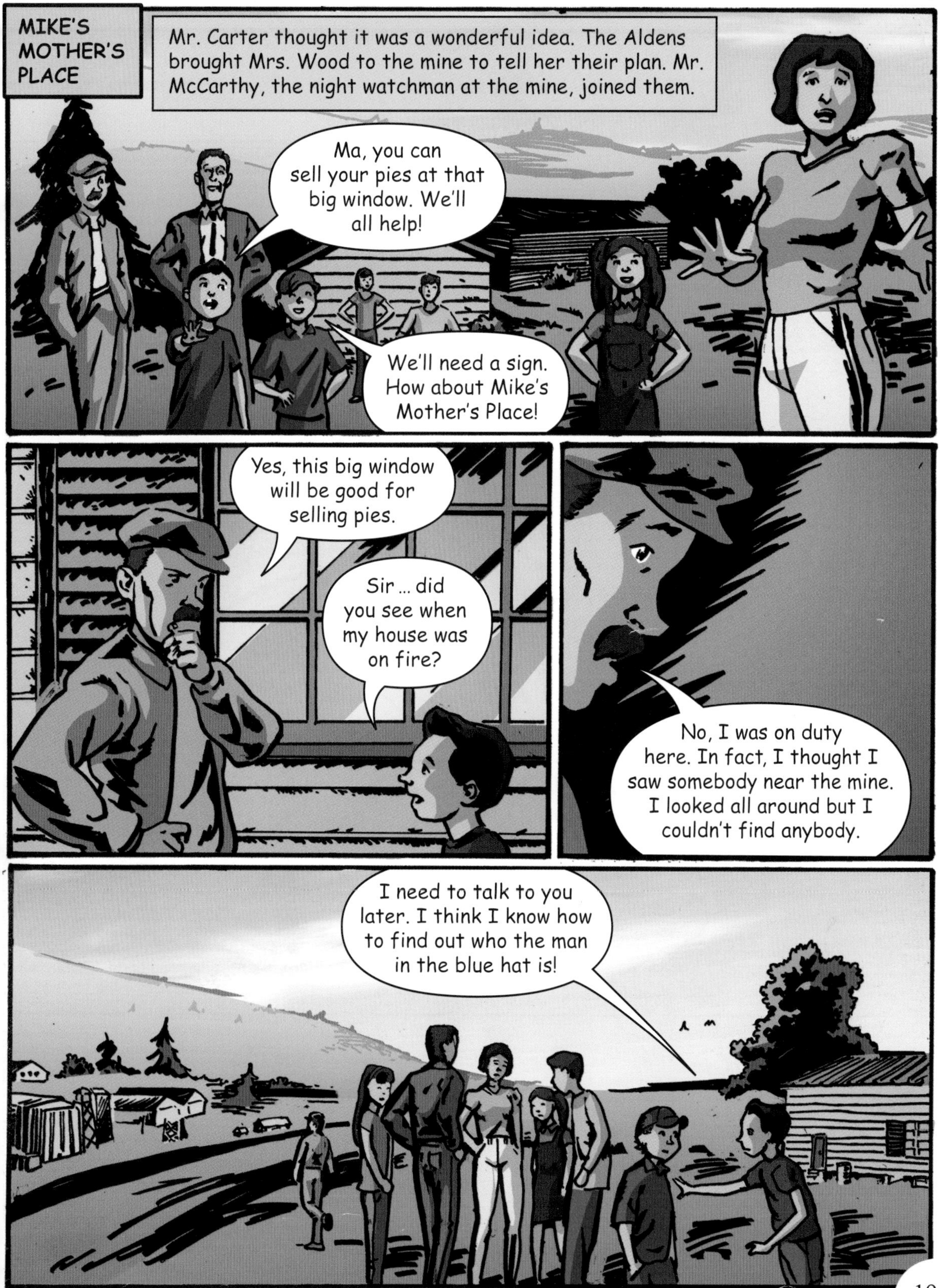
MIKE'S MOTHER'S PLACE
Mr. Carter thought it was a wonderful idea. The Aldens brought Mrs. Wood to the mine to tell her their plan. Mr. McCarthy, the night watchman at the mine, joined them.
Ma, you can sell your pies at that big window. We'll all help!
We'll need a sign. How about Mike's Mother's Place!
Yes, this big window will be good for selling pies.
Sir ... did you see when my house was on fire?
No, I was on duty here. In fact, I thought I saw somebody near the mine. I looked all around but I couldn't find anybody.
I need to talk to you later. I think I know how to find out who the man in the blue hat is!

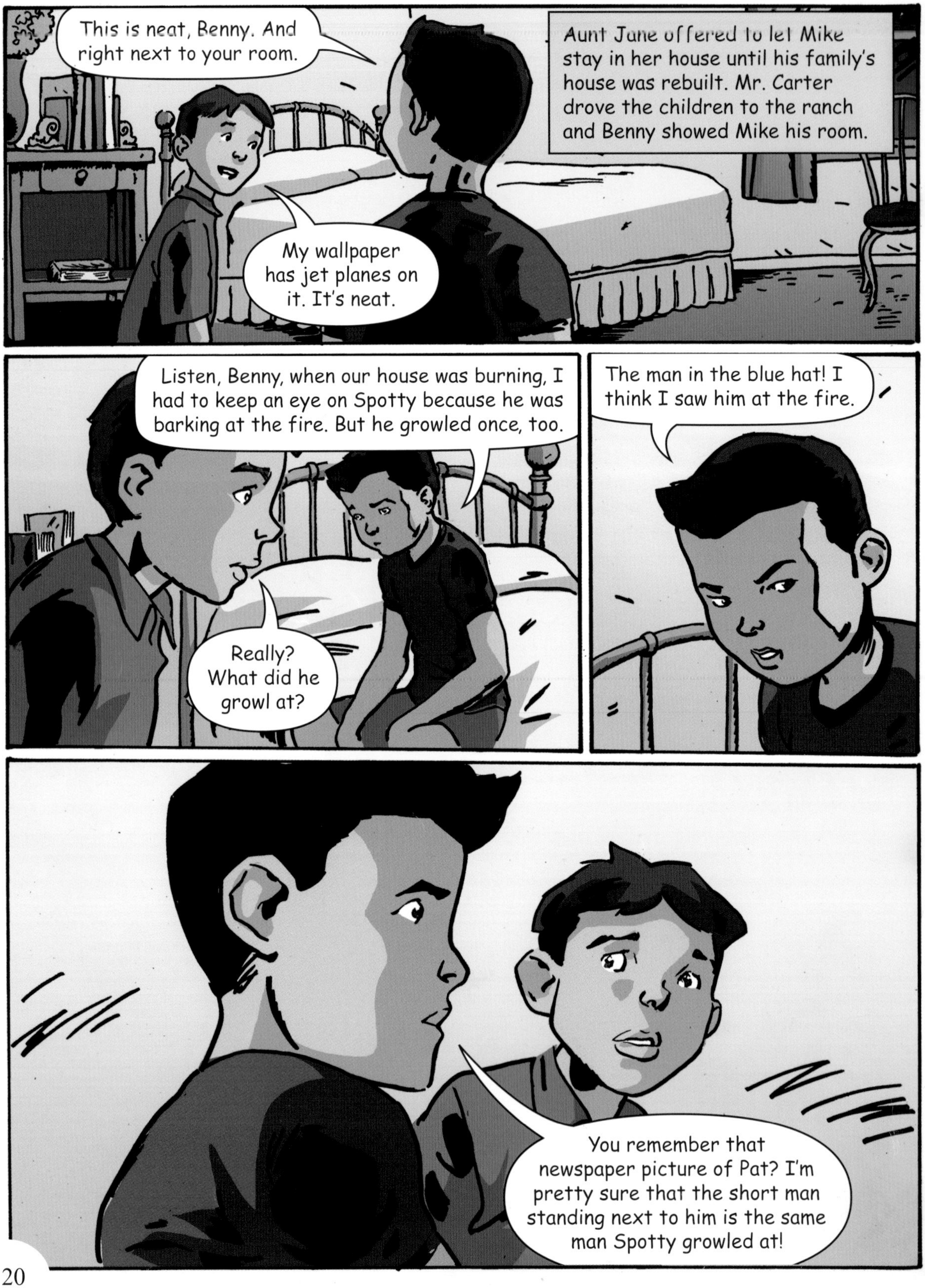
Aunt Jane offered to let Mike stay in her house until his family's house was rebuilt. Mr. Carter drove the children to the ranch and Benny showed Mike his room.
This is neat, Benny. And right next to your room.
My wallpaper has jet planes on it. It's neat.
Listen, Benny, when our house was burning, I had to keep an eye on Spotty because he was barking at the fire. But he growled once, too.
Really? What did he growl at?
The man in the blue hat! I think I saw him at the fire.
You remember that newspaper picture of Pat? I'm pretty sure that the short man standing next to him is the same man Spotty growled at!

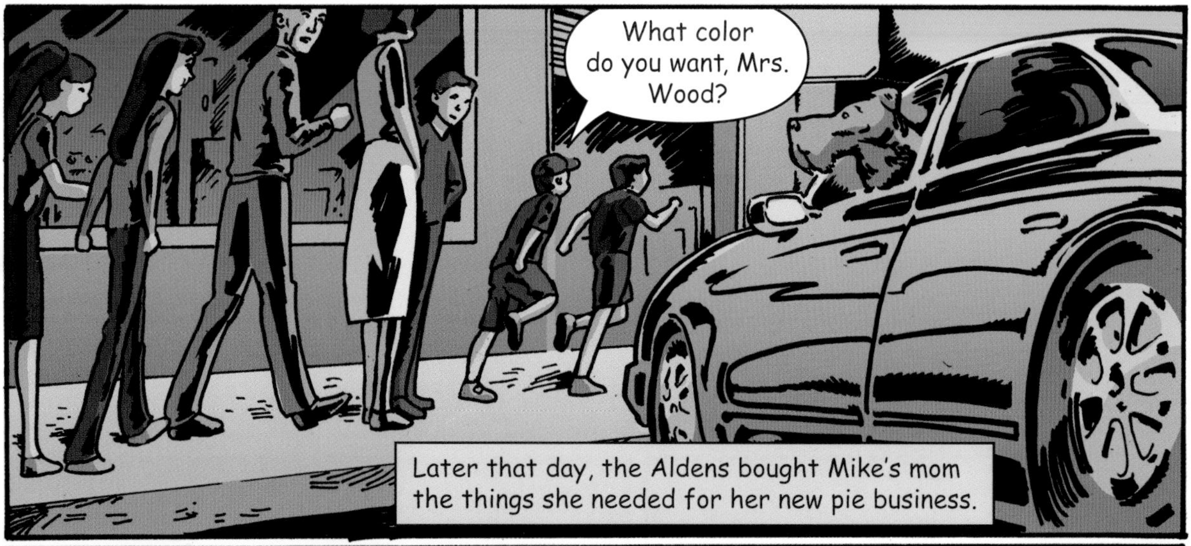
What color do you want, Mrs. Wood?
Later that day, the Aldens bought Mike's mom the things she needed for her new pie business.

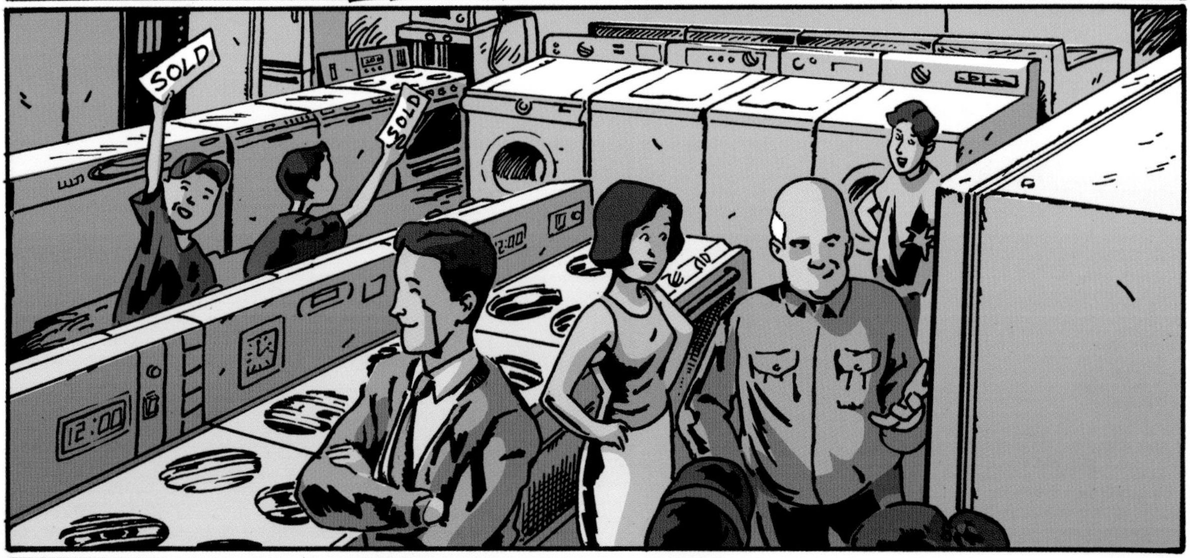
SOLD
SOLD
12:00
12:00

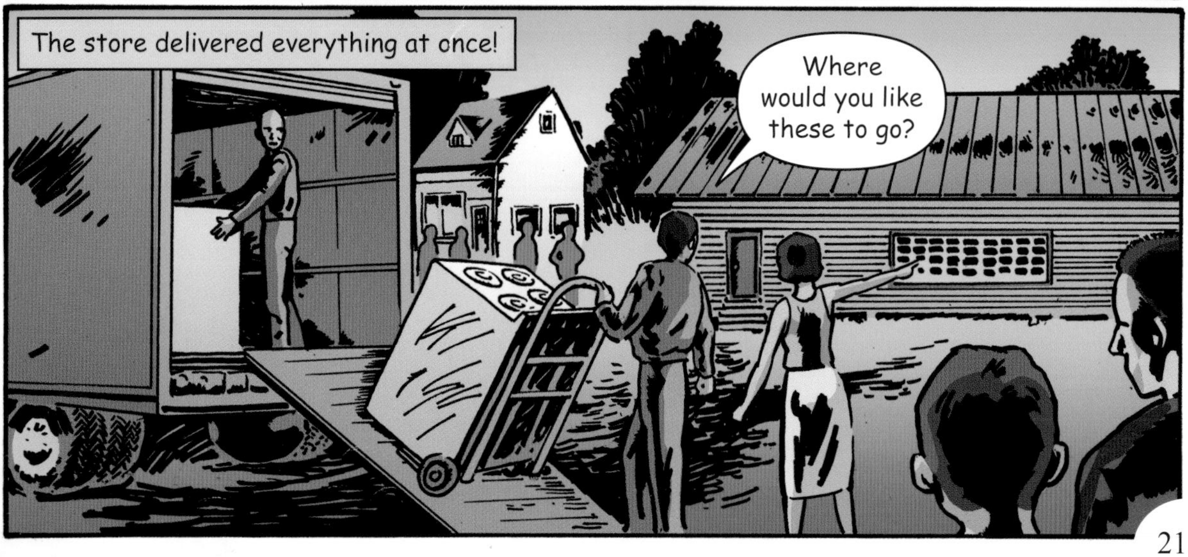
The store delivered everything at once!
Where would you like these to go?

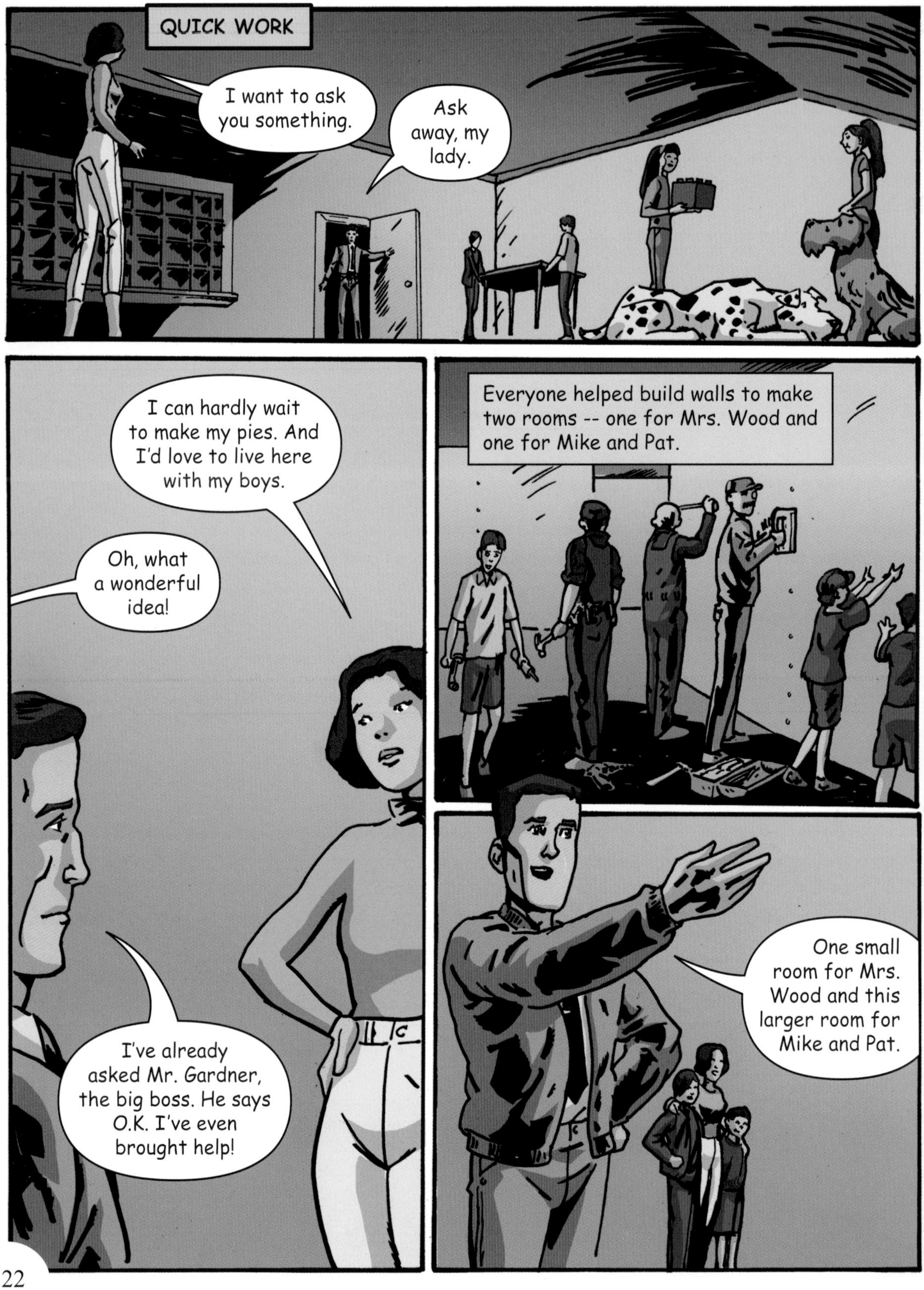
QUICK WORK
I want to ask you something.
Ask away, my lady.
I can hardly wait to make my pies. And I'd love to live here with my boys.
Oh, what a wonderful idea!
I've already asked Mr. Gardner, the big boss. He says O.K. I've even brought help!
Everyone helped build walls to make two rooms -- one for Mrs. Wood and one for Mike and Pat.
One small room for Mrs. Wood and this larger room for Mike and Pat.

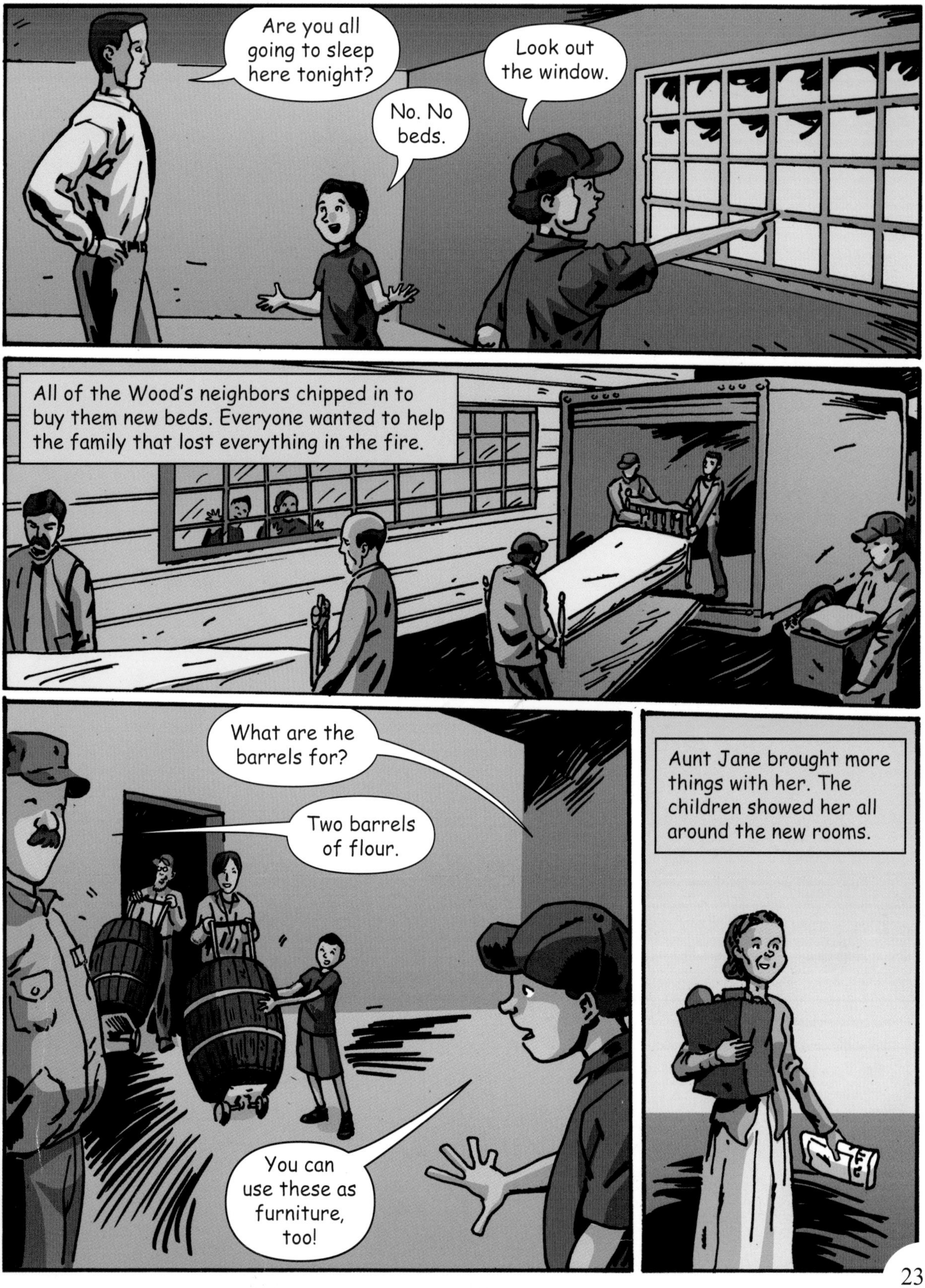
Are you all going to sleep here tonight?
No. No beds.
Look out the window.
All of the Wood's neighbors chipped in to buy them new beds. Everyone wanted to help the family that lost everything in the fire.
What are the barrels for?
Two barrels of flour.
You can use these as furniture, too!
Aunt Jane brought more things with her. The children showed her all around the new rooms.

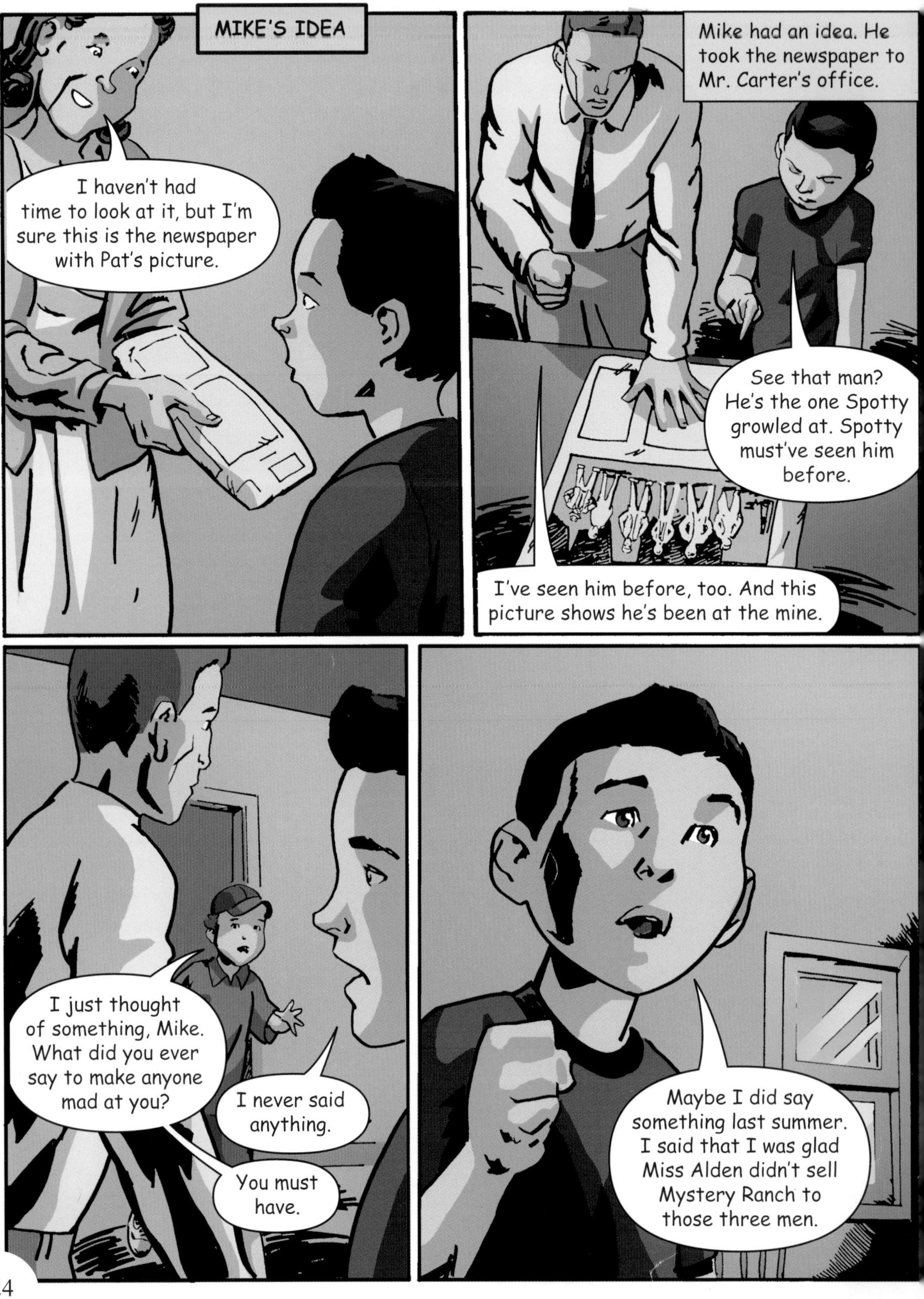
MIKE'S IDEA
I haven't had time to look at it, but I'm sure this is the newspaper with Pat's picture.
Mike had an idea. He took the newspaper to Mr. Carter's office.
See that man? He's the one Spotty growled at. Spotty must've seen him before.
I've seen him before, too. And this picture shows he's been at the mine.
I just thought of something, Mike. What did you ever say to make anyone mad at you?
I never said anything.
You must have.
Maybe I did say something last summer. I said that I was glad Miss Alden didn't sell Mystery Ranch to those three men.

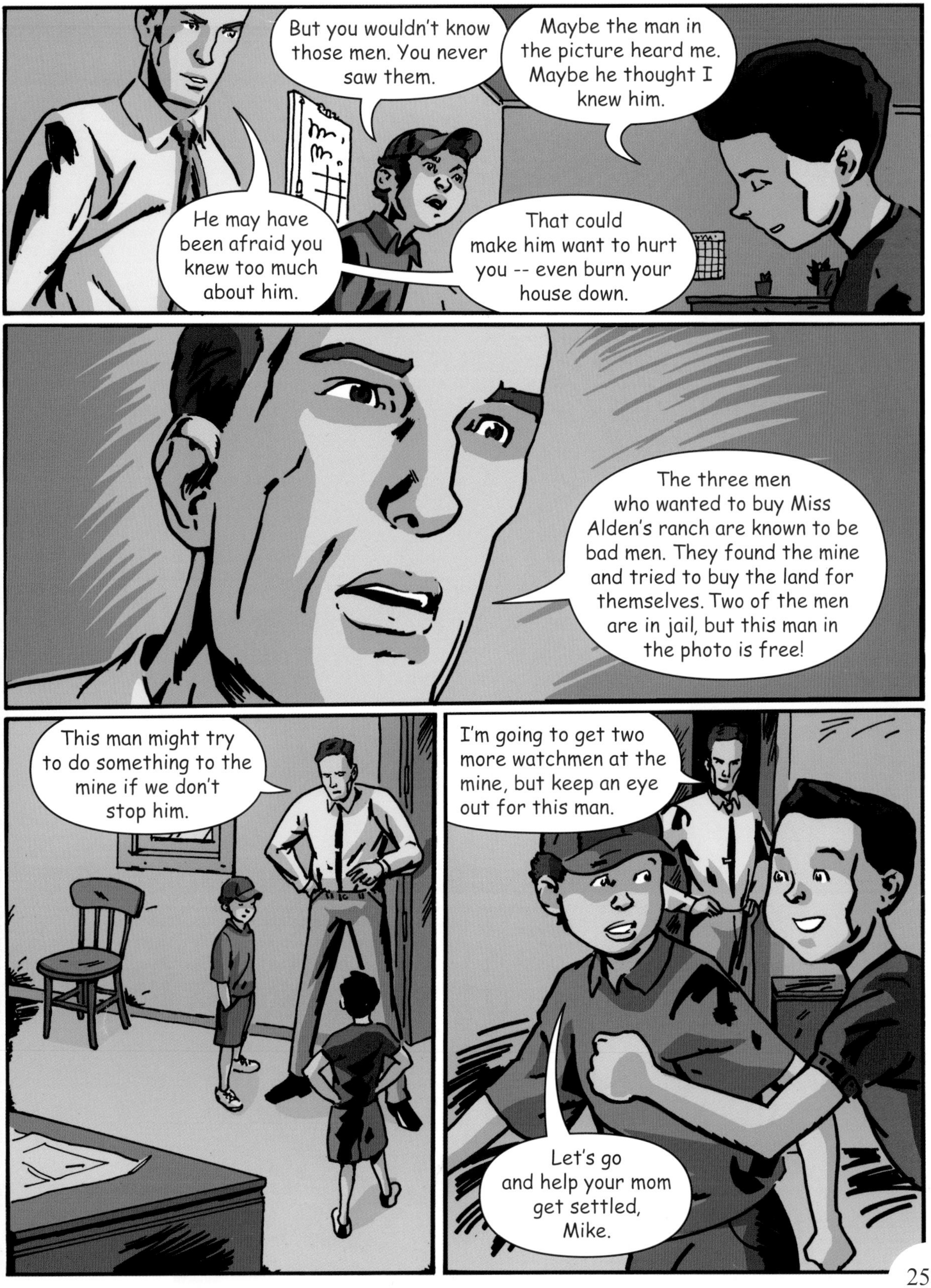
But you wouldn't know those men. You never saw them.
Maybe the man in the picture heard me. Maybe he thought I knew him.
He may have been afraid you knew too much about him.
That could make him want to hurt you -- even burn your house down.
The three men who wanted to buy Miss Alden's ranch are known to be bad men. They found the mine and tried to buy the land for themselves. Two of the men are in jail, but this man in the photo is free!
This man might try to do something to the mine if we don't stop him.
I'm going to get two more watchmen at the mine, but keep an eye out for this man.
Let's go and help your mom get settled, Mike.

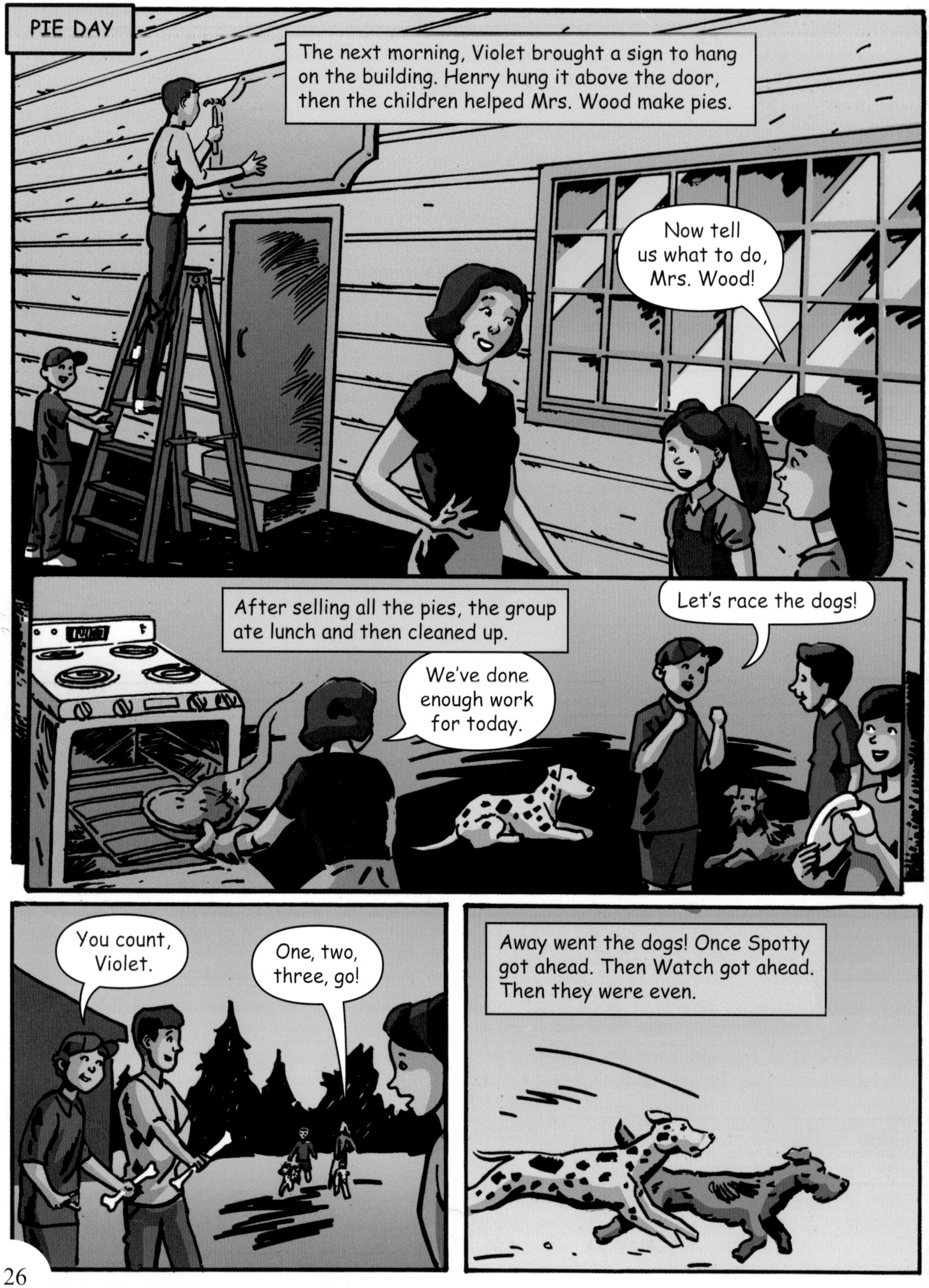
PIE DAY
The next morning, Violet brought a sign to hang on the building. Henry hung it above the door, then the children helped Mrs. Wood make pies.
Now tell us what to do, Mrs. Wood!
After selling all the pies, the group ate lunch and then cleaned up.
We've done enough work for today.
Let's race the dogs!
You count, Violet.
One, two, three, go!
Away went the dogs! Once Spotty got ahead. Then Watch got ahead. Then they were even.

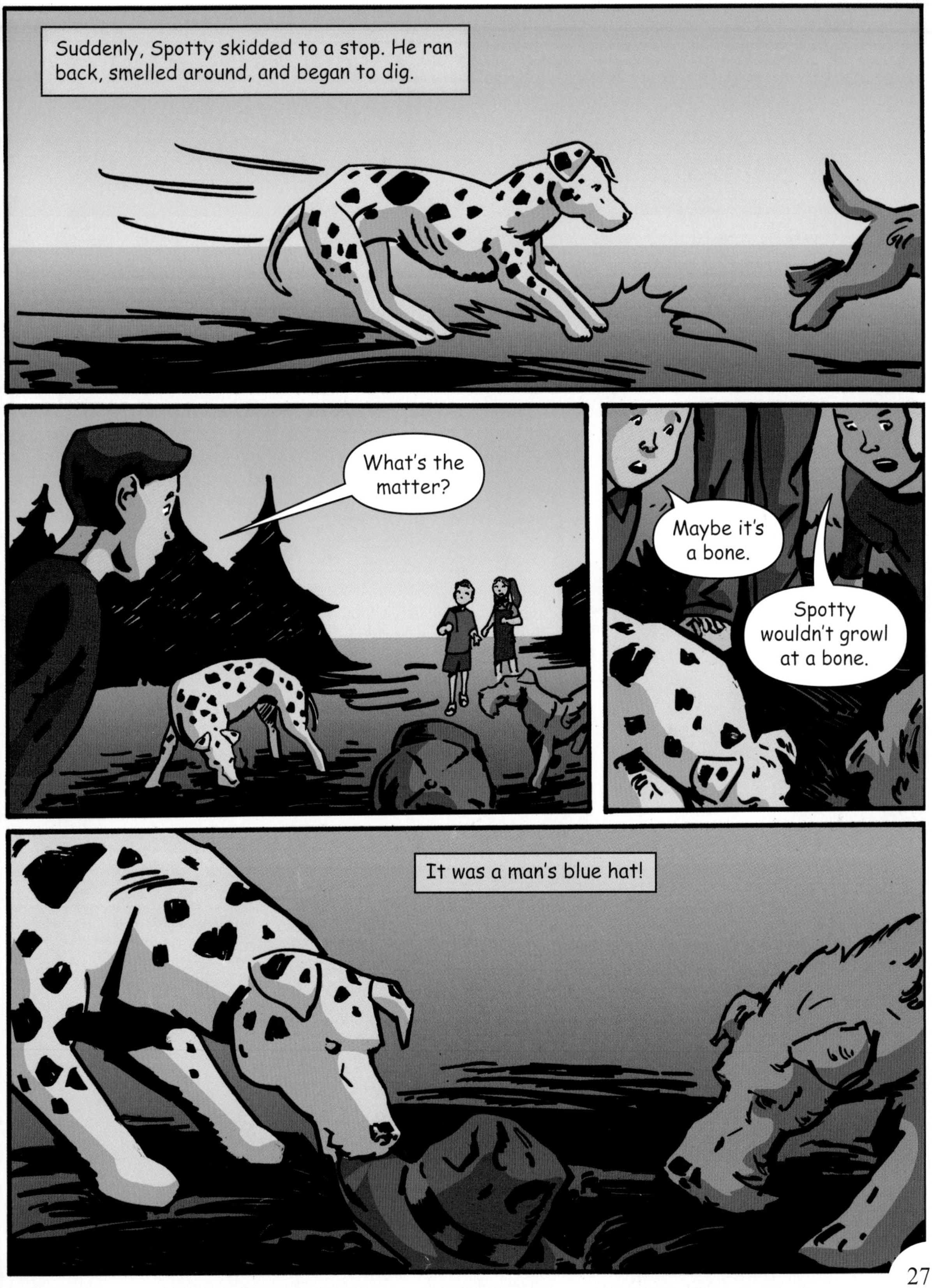
Suddenly, Spotty skidded to a stop. He ran back, smelled around, and began to dig.
What's the matter?
Maybe it's a bone.
Spotty wouldn't growl at a bone.
It was a man's blue hat!

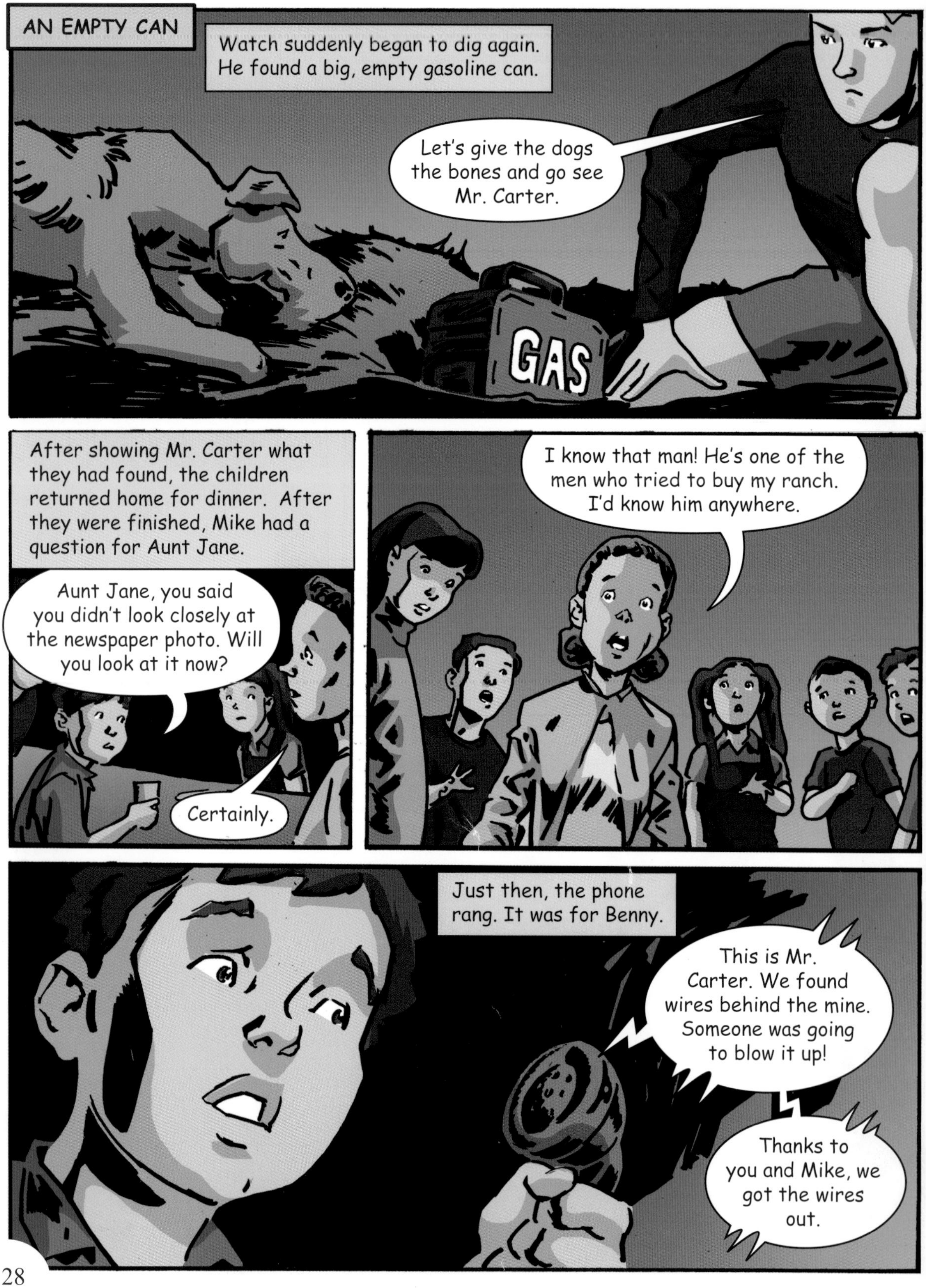
AN EMPTY CAN
Watch suddenly began to dig again. He found a big, empty gasoline can.
Let's give the dogs the bones and go see Mr. Carter.
GAS
After showing Mr. Carter what they had found, the children returned home for dinner. After they were finished, Mike had a question for Aunt Jane.
Aunt Jane, you said you didn't look closely at the newspaper photo. Will you look at it now?
Certainly.
I know that man! He's one of the men who tried to buy my ranch. I'd know him anywhere.
Just then, the phone rang. It was for Benny.
This is Mr. Carter. We found wires behind the mine. Someone was going to blow it up!
Thanks to you and Mike, we got the wires out.

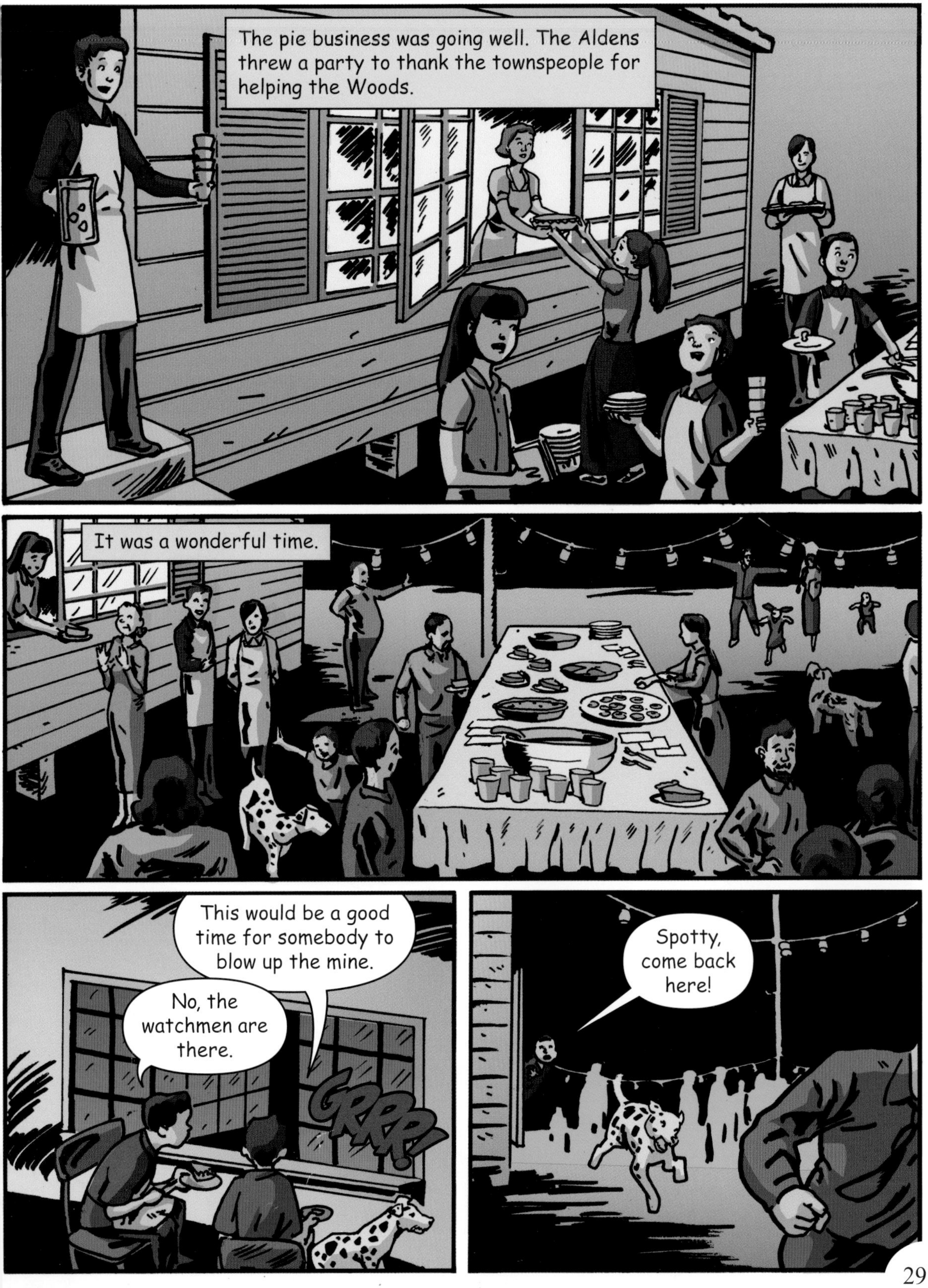

The pie business was going well. The Aldens threw a party to thank the townspeople for helping the Woods.
It was a wonderful time.
This would be a good time for somebody to blow up the mine.
No, the watchmen are there.
GRRR!
Spotty, come back here!

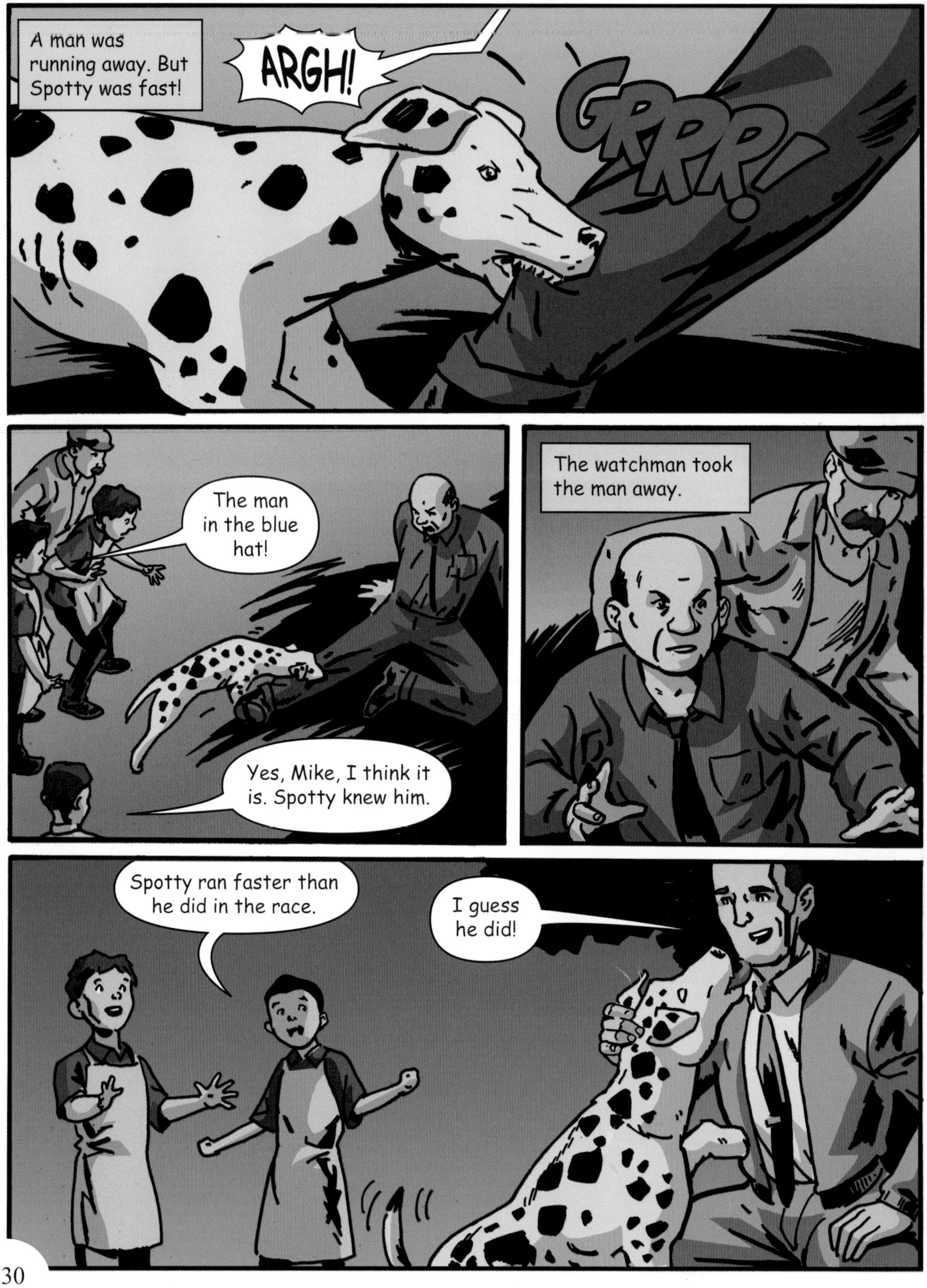
A man was running away. But Spotty was fast!
ARGH!
GRRR!
The man in the blue hat!
Yes, Mike, I think it is. Spotty knew him.
The watchman took the man away.
Spotty ran faster than he did in the race.
I guess he did!

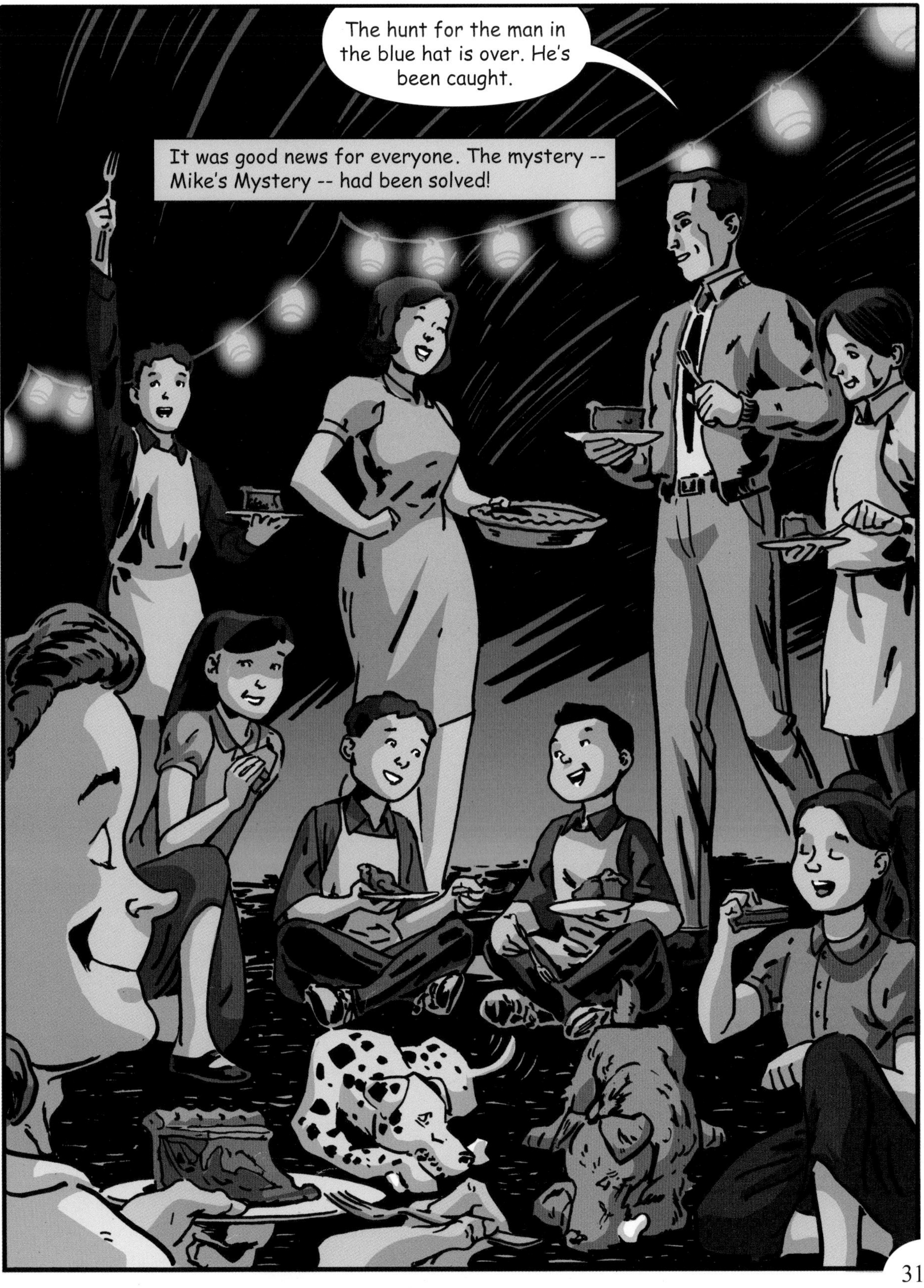

The hunt for the man in the blue hat is over. He's been caught.
It was good news for everyone. The mystery -- Mike's Mystery -- had been solved!

ABOUT THE CREATOR

Gertrude Chandler Warner was born on April 16, 1890, in Putnam, Connecticut. In 1918, Warner began teaching at Israel Putnam School. As a teacher, she discovered that many readers who liked an exciting story could not find books that were both easy and fun to read. She decided to try to meet this need. In 1942, *The Boxcar Children* was published for these readers.

Warner drew on her own experience to write *The Boxcar Children*. As a child she spent hours watching trains go by on the tracks near her family home. She often dreamed about what it would be like to live in a caboose or freight car—just as the Alden children do.

When readers asked for more Alden adventures, Warner began additional stories. While the mystery element is central to each of the books, she never thought of them as strictly juvenile mysteries. She liked to stress the Aldens' independence. Henry, Jessie, Violet, and Benny go about most of their adventures with as little adult supervision as possible—something that delights young readers.

During her lifetime, Warner received hundreds of letters from fans as she continued the Aldens' adventures, writing nineteen Boxcar Children books in all. After her death in 1979, her publisher, Albert Whitman and Company, carried on Warner's vision. Today, the Boxcar Children series has more than 100 books.